Watch for the Jaguar

Watch for the Jaguar

by

Virgil Oglesby

RIVERCROSS PUBLISHING, Inc.
Orlando

ISBN: 1-58141-014-X

Library of Congress Catalog Card Number: 99–055108

First Printing

Library of Congress Cataloging-in-Publication Data

Oglesby, Virgil, 1929–
     Watch for the jaguar / by Virgil Oglesby.
         p. cm
     ISBN 1–58141–014–x
     1. Drug traffic—South America—Fiction. 2. Government investigators—United States—Fiction. I. Title.

PS3565.G4495 W38 1999
813'.54—dc21
                                                                99–055108

Many thanks to my good friend,
LTC KENNETH YENTER, US Army Retired.
His more than twenty years in military
intelligence provided me with valuable
insight and assistance.

Special thanks to
my loving and devoted
wife, Grace who has
given me much help
and encouragement.

To my son, Scott, who
has been a great inspiration
to me

NEVER SHARE A FOXHOLE WITH ANYONE BRAVER
THAN YOU
Rule 6 - Murphy's Laws of Combat

ONE

The Greater the Power, the more dangerous the abuse.

Edmund Burke, 1771

The craggy–featured, well–built man, with dirty blond hair, several inches over six feet, got out of a small, ten-year-old car, possibly European built. With him were two burly younger men, watchful and alert.

They had landed in a small private jet at Buga, Columbia in South America. They had been picked up and driven to the small adobe villa-style house surrounded by encroaching jungle. Bougainvilla blossoms grew over the corner of the house but even the fragrance of their blossoms could not overcome the smell of verdant jungle. The continuous squawking of the jungle birds were the only sounds heard except for the crunch of the men's footsteps on the gravel path as they walked to the building.

They entered a courtyard and were met by a swarthy skinned, hispanic individual and two others. They shook hands all around and sat down at a table right there in the courtyard.

The three new arrivals were CIA agents; the craggy–faced one, the leader, was called the Striker. The other two were the muscle or bodyguards.

11

The hispanic men were high ranking members of the Medellin Cartel, the major drug manufacturing and smuggling group in South America. A few minutes after their discussion began two waiters appeared with cold drinks. Talk immediately stopped. The craggy–faced big man reached under his jacket, pulled out an almost standard CIA issue, long barrel, .32 caliber pistol, silencer already screwed on, and calmly shot the first waiter in the head. As the younger one turned to run he carefully lined up the sights and squeezed the trigger and the running boy, for he wasn't even a grown man, fell forward, a bullet wound in the back of his head.

Both men accompanying the Striker had risen. Both had Uzi's out covering the cartel men.

The Striker said, "I told you. Only you and two others; no one else, not even servants. Are there any others? Quick, before we kill you all."

"No, senor, they were only my servants and no one else is around. There was no reason for you to kill them."

"No, Miguel, *you* killed them by having them here. Now, do we continue or is this meeting over?"

"We continue, senor. But first I will have the bodies removed." He nodded. The two men with him dragged the bodies into the house, then returned. All sat down and the weapons disappeared.

The discussion that followed essentially confirmed an on-going agreement that CIA aircraft would make eighteen deliveries to the Los Angeles International Airport during the following six months.

Each delivery would consist of one thousand kilos of the cartel's best product, or two thousand two hundred pounds of the white powder. In return the agency would pay $2.78 million in cash at the delivery point for each of the eighteen deliveries. The net amount of a little over fifty million dollars would go into an account to finance the Contras war in Nicaragua against the Sandinistas.

The cartel members were pleased at the results of this meeting as they had expected to be asked to more than double the previous price of $2.5 million for each trip. Some two hours later the meeting concluded and the Americans were driven back to the Buga Airport where the private jet was waiting to whisk them to their home base in Panama.

Back at the villa the swarthy hispanic was cursing in Spanish and vowing to bring the "dirty gringo to his knees." His two companions joined their boss in pledging to get the gringo Striker in their clutches.

To someone not familiar with the clandestine operations of the United States Central Intelligence Agency (CIA), the foregoing account would be considered outlandish and even un-believable; however, there are those who are so mission-oriented that any means justifies their ends.

The CIA is compartmentalized into missions, with many compartments and sub-compartments. There are desk officers within each compartment; operators or field agents who go out to do the Agency's intelligence gathering; counter-intelligence and dirty-trick actions. To imagine the very worst things that might happen would not be half as bad as the reality of the way the agency operates.

TWO

"I can resist everything except temptation."
Oscar Wilde

John Henry Clay stared at the chief, so called because of his rank of Chief Warrant Officer, fixed wing and rotary qualified aircraft flyer in that long ago war in Vietnam. He sat in a soft lounge chair, almost reclining, and looked fixedly at the chief who sat with his feet propped up on the coffee table in front of him.

The chief was a slightly pudgy, average height, open-faced man of about 175 pounds, with sandy light-brown hair. His name was Thomas E. Thompson, and he and Clay went back about twenty-four years having met the first time in late 1964 in 'nam.

Clay was bleary-eyed, having helped the chief and several of his co-workers scarf down ten pisgah sours, the drink of choice in South America.

It wasn't only the booze that had Clay bleary-eyed but also the high altitude.

That afternoon at about 1400 hours, he had off loaded from the chief's aircraft at El Alto airport, the world's highest commercial airport at 13,358 feet above sea level.

Clay had run into the chief in Santiago, Chile, and hitched a ride with him to La Paz, Bolivia, their RON or

14

Remain Over Night stop in his round-robin run for the company around the capitals of South America.

Clay was hoping to get back to the states, as circumstances had left him stony broke a long way from home.

The chief had taken him in tow in El Alto. After securing the C-130 aircraft the group had proceeded to La Paz, some 12,000 feet above sea level. At that altitude smokers and bad lung people have to carry a "green bottle" of oxygen to help their oxygen–starved bodies. Any exertion brought quick chest pains and a tiredness almost beyond belief.

Once in La Paz, the entire group immediately began some heavy drinking at the little bar and supper club on the fourth floor, the top floor, where all their rooms were located.

What the chief had just told Clay was not surprising. In Vietnam the chief had flown for Air America also known as the company or in plainer terms, the Central Intelligence Agency, or simply the CIA, or the agency.

He had just told Clay that he was still with the agency, and had been all this time.

All evening the chief had been trying to convince Clay to join the group he was hauling for. Clay quickly figured out it was a massive drug smuggling operation and told him, and any of the others who were near enough to hear, that despite his drinking and his current financial embarrassment, he was not interested in moving the "death of choice," white powder, into the U.S.

What the chief had just said shocked Clay. If what he had been telling Clay all evening was true then the agency was in the drug smuggling business big time.

He shook his head as he looked at Tommy, the chief, Thompson, flyer extraordinaire of any and all kinds of aircraft.

"Chief, is what you're saying true?" he asked. "Is the agency into moving drugs?"

The chief looked around guiltily, and said, "Let's go to your room, John Henry, and talk," and he half pulled and guided Clay out the door and down the hall to Clay's room.

Once inside, the chief said, "John Henry, I've talked too much, but with your run of bad luck I figured you'd jump at the chance to get in on this. You could sock away a million, maybe two or three, in a couple of years." His earnest face had a troubled expression and he fumbled into his flight suit for a cigarette, but put the pack away as he realized he was in Clay's room, and Clay was a dedicated non-smoker.

He paused, then said, "I should have known better 'cause I've known you since you were in the Forces in 'nam—what year was that, 64 or 65?—and you've never been interested in anything except the army, God and your country, and not necessarily in that order. Well," he continued, "I've screwed up, big time, ole' buddy, so now I've got to figure a way out for you." He had commenced pacing the small room but stopped to look out the window at the evening traffic and the people hurrying down the street.

He turned to face Clay, and went on. "I'm okay, I think, but people will be coming to hire you or silence you, so I'm going to at least try to even it up some when you turn them down. These are bad dudes, Dude."

With that the chief reached into the inside pocket of his flight jacket and pulled out a long barrel, .32 caliber, semi-automatic pistol. He reached into a hip pocket and pulled out a baffled nose screwon silencer. He installed it and handed the pistol to Clay, saying, "John Henry, I'm sorry as hell about this. I got mushy having a few toddys with an old friend and said too much. There's twelve rounds plus one in the chamber and the safety is on." He also pulled some U.S. currency from his pocket and dropped it on the small reading table without counting it. Clay could see several fifties and more twenties and tens in the wadded up roll of money.

Clay said, "Chief, what is this shit? The agency can't be helping smuggle drugs into the U.S."

"Hell, John Henry, it's not smuggling. We just load it up and fly it in the west coast, usually L.A. Then a big truck meets us and hauls it off. It's a secret operation. No customs people ever come around. The proceeds from the cargo are put into a numbered account in a Swiss Bank. Then our people, under President Reagan before and now under President Bush, use it to pay for the Contras' battles in Nicaragua."

He went on, "Congress pulled the rug from under us, so now we're selling arms, tanks, and planes that are newer and in better condition than what our own GIs have to use, to get money to fight this war. Hell, John Henry, it's common knowledge. Why are you so surprised?

"Look" he went on, "there's a C-130 that makes an embassy run from Panama to all these little countries down here. Be at the airport at 1100 hours tomorrow and I'll have you flown back to Panama on it. That's the best I can do for you, John Henry," and he left Clay there, drunk and very confused.

17

THREE

After the event, even a fool is wise.
Homer (Iliad)

John Henry Clay was from Kentucky, and according to some family members, a distant relative of the famous orator and statesman from Kentucky, Henry Clay. Now approaching forty he was, according to his ex-wife, a flop and a failure at everything.

John Henry Clay stood six feet two inches tall and weighed a firm 220 pounds. He was athletically built and clean cut. But his unique features were his eyes. They were a penetrating light gray that seemed to bore through people and see everything at a glance. He was a sport star in high school and was offered several small college football scholarships. He visited one campus, but was uncomfortable with the shallow people he met and opted to work for an uncle who had a small farm equipment store. This uncle preached "duty, honor and country" to John Henry for over a year and a half, a lecture that only ended when he left to join the army at twenty years of age.

Once in the army he fooled around for a couple of years then woke up one day and said, "Hell, why not?" and put in a form 1049 requesting Officer Candidate School.

18

He was accepted and sent to Fort Benning, Georgia to attend the Infantry School's Officer Candidate School. After John Henry received a commission as a Second Lieutenant of Infantry, United States Army, he was immediately sent to the Infantry School's Officer's Basic Course. While in the Basic Course Clay applied for and was accepted for parachute jump school. He followed this with Special Warfare School and upon graduation received an assignment to Special Forces.

John Henry sailed through jump school and the Special Warfare School and found he loved not only parachuting but the adventure and challenges of Special Forces.

As the second officer of an FA team after graduation Clay practiced long hours learning each and every function of the ten enlisted positions in the team.

In 1964 the team transferred to Okinawa from the Seventh Group to the Fifth Special Forces Group, and the training continued, only now for Vietnam. A team would be deployed to 'nam for six months then back to the Fifth SF Group for more training, and more importantly to pass on to new teams what they had learned.

While in Okinawa Clay enrolled in off-duty martial arts training, featuring jiujitsu, the Japanese form of unarmed combat. There, he startled the instructors with how quickly he assimilated it, and by his quickness and balance. In a very short time none of the instructors had anything further to teach or show him.

Militarily, he moved through the ranks on time, but had not one promotion below the zone. His promotions, in other words, were on time and on track with the infantry branch career patterns, until as a major he entered the zone for promotion to lieutenant colonel during his fourteenth year of service. He failed to be selected despite two Silver

Stars, three Purple Hearts, and more Bronze Star Medals than he could remember.

He was a B-Team commander by then and one day over a cold beer asked the group commander what could be the problem, as he'd seen every efficiency report made on him and they were all top-notch. The colonel drew him a diagram of a pyramid on a bar napkin and explained that the peak left about 60% of good officers out at that point. Further with only thirteen years in the forces he had not "experienced" all the "career broadening" jobs, staff and otherwise, of his career group so according to the system of selecting upper field grades he was judged lacking. Because the selection board had to cut out sixty percent of otherwise good officers it looked for the six out of ten to turn down rather than for the best officers to promote.

The colonel added, "John Henry, don't worry, you'll make it next time. You're the best officer I've ever served with."

Clay buckled down and crossed every "t" and dotted every "i" but when another selection board met fifteen months later he was not selected. Shortly afterward he received a notice of "involuntary separation" from the service based on "non-selection" for Lieutenant Colonel, and ninety days later John Henry Clay was a civilian with sixteen and one half wasted years.

The ensuing drunken binge lasted five years and resulted in a divorce and limited visitation for him to see his one child, John Henry, Jr.

The binge might have lasted longer but an acute "lack of funds" suddenly reared its ugly head and John Henry was in danger of not being able to make his child support payments.

Since his qualifications for jobs in civilian life were limited to the mafia, Clay took short term and undesirable work until a hispanic business man he met in Miami hired him to provide protection for his wife who was taking a two to three week trip to South America.

His pay was twenty-five hundred dollars a week plus expenses with five thousand dollars up front. There was a $10,000.000 minimum as well.

His bodyguarding stint lasted three weeks, with him having to fight off the wife's advances nightly until she found someone more willing in Santiago, Chile, her original home.

The suitor, a wealthy property owner, and a second cousin of the cheating wife, made it known he would tolerate no interference. After some six hours at the telephone trying to reach his employer to find out how far he wanted Clay to go to "protect" his interests, he was summarily fired and told to forget the balance of his fee despite the fact there had been no mention of protecting the woman's chastity.

Clay vowed to collect the balance of his fee later, but having paid his child support and past due bills with the upfront money he was now in South America almost stone broke.

On top of these problems Clay had been not only recruited to run drugs but had been warned by the chief that by refusing those overtures he was in danger of being silenced.

In his drunken stupor Clay had a problem putting it all together. Thinking water might help he dunked himself into a tepid bath. Coming out of the bath in his "oriental" robe he looked the pistol over, noting the side thumb safety, then put it in the right hand side pocket of his robe. Then he went to bed and lay there remembering how he had met the chief.

FOUR

*Yea, though we walk through the valley of the shadow
of death, we fear no evil, for we're the meanest sons-
of-bitches in the valley.*
Special Forces Prayer

September 1964. Immediately following the formation
of the Fifth Special Forces Group rear headquarters at Okinawa and forward headquarters in the central highlands
of South Vietnam, later to be designated U.S. Forces, II
Corps, John Henry Clay as second officer, and now a first
lieutenant of A-273, was deployed to South Vietnam in a
border screening mission, with base camp at Plei Nam,
South Vietnam.

There were 168 LLDBs or "Luc-Luong Dac Biet," the
Vietnamese name for the Army of the Republic of Vietnam
(ARVN) Special Forces, 116 CIDG, or Civilian Irregular Defense Group, hired and trained to defend their own areas
against the Viet Cong.

In addition, Captain Roger Golden, the team leader,
had "hired" twelve Nungs, mercenaries of Chinese extrac-
tion he had known from previous tours, and arranged to
have them flown in with the team.

There was also a ARVN artillery section of two guns,
105mm artillery pieces, with 38 men assigned to it. The

team also had two interpreters and two former Viet Cong who had deserted to come work for the Special Forces.

During that same period there was a revolution of the Montagnards against their Vietnamese masters. This uprising was going under the acronym FULRO, a French series of words meaning the Front to Free the Oppressed Peoples, in this case, the Montagnards.

All the CIDG were Yards and all the LLDB (Viet Special Forces) were Vietnamese. There was a lot of animosity but due primarily to Captain Golden's motivational and excellent negotiating skills the CIDG stayed in place with the team, rather than leaving to join the other Montagnards marching on Ban me thuot.

The camp was set up in a huge triangle with an outer ring of barbed wire, called concertina wire, and mines. There was an inner ring of barbed wire in front of the bunker line, which all mutually supported with their weapons.

In addition there was a second camp within the large camp, which included the mortar positions, team communications bunker, six sleeping bunkers, four ammo bunkers, a cook bunker or mess area, a watch tower and a supply bunker. Running to the north toward the south end of the airfield which entered the wire of the outer ring at that point, was the ARVN Artillery.

Although there had been minor contacts with the local Viet Cong (VC) no major attacks took place until late November, when after two days of heavy overcast and monsoon rain, a major assault was launched by the 61st Sao Vang main force regiment.

The attack commenced at 0100 hours with a heavy mortar barrage and ground assault on the western perimeter and several strange things occurred, or at least they seemed strange to John Henry.

First, after a few volleys of small arms fire from the village on the west, the normally reliable CIDGs broke and ran to the opening in the wire on the north near the air strip. This all occurred just a few minutes before the all-out assault on the west side.

Also just prior to the all-out attack two ammo bunkers blew up, lighting up the camp as if it were day.

As the Americans and their Nung mercenaries rushed to their fighting positions a well–aimed burst of fire from the watch tower struck and killed Captain Golden and seriously wounded the team sergeant and a Nung who was with them.

John Henry flattened out against the wall of the trench and guided a long burst of .45 caliber Thompson sub-machine gun fire to the tower. Two screaming LLDBs fell to the ground. Another LLDB soldier was firing on the Tactical Operations Center (TOC) and John Henry "hosed" him and blew him off the berm.

Clay called for a medic but could see as he passed the team commander that he was dead. He and his Nung and one of the weapons men hurried to the mortar fighting position. The four Nungs assigned to the tubes immediately settled down with the Americans and commenced putting out accurate fire on the assaulting Cong who were trying to breach the western perimeter.

The illumination was poor, being only from the white phosphorus grenades set in the wire and triggered off by trip wires. But the relatively few LLDB who could be seen were breaking and running, leaving their positions.

Clay yelled to the Nungs on the mortars to make every third round from the 81mm mortars a flair round. Soon the entire western perimeter was illuminated. As the Nungs and Americans began to blast huge holes in the advancing enemy, the CIDGs went forward into the bunkers left open by the LLDBs. The line was holding.

Isolated enemy squads and some occasional LLDB turncoats who were showing their true colors, made movement from one position to another extremely dangerous.

Clay estimated a full twenty-five percent of the LLDBs had turned out to be Viet Cong, but apparently the CIDGs who had run to the openings in the wire at the onset were only concerned about their families. They were returning. The battle continued to rage with Clay trying to be in all places at the same time. He finally ran completely out of ammo and grenades in encounters between bunkers.

He made it to the commo bunker, killing two VC and a "cross-over" LLDB who were trying to roll stick grenades into the bunker.

Clay yelled that he was coming in and waited until he got an okay then entered the "commo shack."

The communications sergeant had the B Team on the radio and was told that all aircraft were grounded due to heavy weather and rain.

Clay had checked the ammo bunkers and knew small arms ammo and grenades were getting dangerously low. He also knew that at the rate it was being expended they would be completely out before daylight.

John Henry told the commo sergeant to continue trying to get relief or resupply. Then, taking a fresh supply of ammo and several grenades, he headed back out into the chaos as the Americans, Nungs, and CIDG fought a see-saw battle for control of the camp.

Clay found Captain Lam cowering in the LLDB TOC but could not get a coherent report from him so he turned to the LLDB Sergeant Major who appeared to be controlling the troops still in their fighting positions.

Getting off his land-line the sergeant turned to Clay, ignoring his commander crouched against the wall of the bunker. "Trung-Wei, it is very bad. More than thirty percent of our soldiers were secretly Viet Cong. We are isolating them and killing them but we are getting very low on ammunition. Three of our own men blew up two ammunition bunkers, and the CIDG have taken over the other two and refuse us resupply. We must have ammunition and grenades immediately."

"Roger that, Trung-Sat, we are in contact with the B team and hope to get resupplied soon. I'll get the CIDG to give you ammo." With that Clay left the LLDB TOC to find out why the CIDG had taken over the ammo bunkers.

Clay killed two more LLDBs who had fired on him when he'd left their Command Post (CP). Again, his fast reactions had allowed him to return accurate and deadly fire as he moved through the trench network.

Clay arrived at the first ammo bunker at the same time as Lieutenant Lieu, the commander of the CIDG forces. He received and returned a quick salute while noting a squad of Montagnard troops guarding the ammo bunker entrance.

Clay pointed to the troops and said, "It's a good idea, to secure the ammo bunker but we must let all our troops have ammo."

The smell of cordite and gun powder permeated the area, along with the smell of human blood wafting through the air as bodies were blown apart and people died.

Two russian–made rocket rounds, called RPGs, landed nearby blowing gravel and dirt over the entire area. The noise was deafening.

Clay and Lieutenant Lieu both ducked. When he raised his head the lieutenant had an expression of fury and hate on his face. "Most of them are VC. We will not give them ammunition, Lieutenant Clay. Please understand, we are fighting for our families; they are buffalo dung and most are Communist Cong" he spat contemptuously.

He watched Clay through narrowed eyes. His squad was equally alert and watchful.

"Lieutenant Lieu, I understand, but I say we give ammo to the LLDBs who the Trung Sat says are loyal." Suddenly he pressed his Thompson against the Lieutenant's chest.

The Lieutenant glanced down at Clay's weapon and said, "Lieutenant Clay, you will be killed if you do not lower your weapon."

Clay looked into the man's glittering dark eyes and said, "I'll probably die tonight anyway, Lieutenant, but you will die now, and my Nungs will finish off every man you have here. Our first job is to restore our defensive line and we all must have this ammo."

Lieutenant Lieu looked around, grimaced and said, "All right, Lieutenant Clay. We will issue to everyone."

"Thanks, Lieutenant Lieu," and he shook his hand and turned around and walked away. He could have been shot then but he believed the Lieutenant had seen the wisdom of holding against the VC as first priority.

Clay sent a Nung to tell the LLDB sgt. major ammo would be issued to whomever he sent.

Back at the TOC Clay called out again and was told, "OK to come in" and found the two commo men and one LLDB guard inside. They were still in contact with the B Team.

The commo sergeant reported that all aircraft were still grounded. Clay glanced at his watch. 0400 hours and about two and a half hours until dawn. They would long be out of ammo by then.

27

Then a voice came over the radio, "Hello, Plei Nam, this is your friendly Air America. I've been monitoring your calls for resupply. I have a basic load of small arms ammo, grenades, mortar and other goodies. I have a visual on the camp and most of the runway. Have your people meet me on the south end to off-load and I'll put it as close to your gate as possible. Do you copy? Over."

Clay grabbed the hand-set and answered, "Roger that, Air America. I'm bringing twenty men to that location right now. Over." He handed the mike to the commo sergeant and slammed out the door.

Going by the CIDG TOC he briefly came under fire from the south bunker line but rounded a corner of the trench out of sight and found Lieutenant Lieu. They quickly gathered a group of men and sprinted to the airfield gate. Clay could hear the dual motors of a Gooney Bird up toward the north-end of the runway.

They heard it touch down about midway of the strip and suddenly it was barreling down the runway. Either the pilot had misjudged his touch down or he was having a malfunction of some kind.

He reversed props but was too late to make a clean stop. The C-47 yawed the swung and skidded into the fence line with the tail door only about ten feet from the gate.

The door was pushed open and there stood the pilot, holding the shoulders of his co-pilot, who had been hit. He yelled for help. Clay sprinted to the aircraft and gently lowered the body to the ground, for the man was dead and it was just a body now. The pilot pulled another body to the door, probably the crew chief, and Clay lowered it also. The pilot jumped to the ground and the "Yards" quickly formed a double line and began passing down boxes of ammo and grenades. With a solid line of people passing the eighty pound boxes of ammo into the camp, the aircraft was quickly emptied.

It was not any too soon either as the smoldering plane burst into flames and moments later exploded, throwing hot metal through the air and lighting up the entire south end of the runway and the northern bunker line of the camp. Closing the gates and re-hooking the wire and the claymore mines Clay led the pilot towards the TOC, but was intercepted by the CIDG commander, Lt. Lieu.

"Lt. Clay, the enemy holds seven of the southside bunkers. What must we do?"

"We'll retake them, Lieutenant Lieu. Get me four good men, and Chin and I will go first."

Chin was a Nung who Clay suspected had been told to stay with him and act as a bodyguard. It was sometimes embarrassing to go behind some bushes to answer nature's call and look around and find the tall Nung standing nearby.

They approached the first of the seven bunkers. Clay had men fire on the rear entrances as he and Chin raced close enough to lob grenades in. They followed up with quick bursts of Thompson fire to make sure all were dead.

Fortunately the bunkers were "mutually supporting" only on the front sides, and on the first one Clay noted that in addition to Chin he had the help of the Air America pilot. By having his four man team provide a base of fire after taking each bunker, they quickly routed out the "Dinks" and restored the perimeter.

Chin, Clay and the Air America pilot returned to the CP and at that point Clay and the chief introduced themselves to each other.

Through four or five other tours in 'nam Clay and the chief constantly ran into each other, both working for or under the control of, the agency. They became fast friends and each respected the other's abilities and coolness under fire.

Months later after that fateful night at Plei Nam, Clay found out that on their initial run to bring in the resupply of small arms ammo an enemy fifty-one caliber machine gun had hosed them and killed the crew chief and the copilot. The chief could have aborted and pulled out—but he didn't.

Later, Clay learned from the chief that he was on loan from the U.S. Army to the CIA as a contract pilot. He was making quite a lot of money, in addition to his regular army pay and allowances, and his time was being counted for retirement.

Over the years the chief became more and more closed-mouth with Clay. One time he had intimated that he was not allowed to say anything about what he was doing under penalty of death.

The chief and Clay had become even closer than brothers despite the chief's silence about his work. Clay accepted it and never questioned him about the nature of his assignments, although once the Chief told him that he had no one and had named Clay beneficiary on his SGLI insurance policy.

FIVE

"No bastard ever won a war by dying for his country.
He won it by making the other poor dumb bastard die
for his country.
General George S. Patton Jr.

The following morning Clay showered, shaved and brushed his teeth, and was standing at the window idly watching the early morning traffic down below. He noticed a van with Spanish marking and a picture of a rolled up carpet on the side.

The workers had removed a small roll of carpet and leaned it against the van, but what struck Clay was the watchfulness and alert mien of the two workers, it reminded him of troops preparing to go into action.

As he watched, two other men got out of another small vehicle. They took a long look around and, ignoring the carpet workers, entered the hotel.

The two men who had stood by the roll of carpet and continuously checked their watches, took a final look around. Then they picked up the roll of carpet and entered the hotel. This was definitely a timed operation, and it dawned on Clay they might be people who had come to "reason" with him as the chief had warned.

He quickly moved from the window and stood behind a huge, heavy wooden chiffonier where he could see the door but be somewhat protected. He removed the pistol from the pocket of his robe and flipped the safety down to the off position. No more than twenty seconds later his door burst open and two men charged in, weapons at the ready.

They had silencers on their pistols and Clay noted they appeared to be exact copies of the one he had. The first man spotted Clay and swung his pistol. There was a cough and splinters flew from the corner of the chiffonier. Clay swung his pistol up and fired then swung it toward the other gunman who appeared momentarily unfocused as to where Clay was. Clay's bullet caught him in the forehead and he fell back against the door, pushing it shut.

Clay rushed to the bodies. Both were dead. The smell of powder smoke filled the room as he went through their pockets.

Neither had I.D. But that didn't mean anything as CIA Agents going to eliminate someone routinely go clean, that is, no ID nor other means to identify them as agency.

Clay confiscated sizable amounts of American "green" as well as their .32 caliber semi-automatic pistols with silencers. The men had brought body bags, rubberized bags to transport bodies to the Graves Registration. He thought for a few seconds then quickly inserted one body into each bag, zipped the bags up and quickly took cover again behind the huge chiffonier.

It was a full minute and half before the two "carpet men" pushed open the door and entered the room. They laid out their thin roll of carpet and placed both bagged up bodies on it, they rolled up the carpet, taped it and departed. It took them about 30 seconds total and they weren't any further than ten steps into the room. Had they checked the area and found him he would have killed them as well, for Clay had a great dislike for people who were using him as a target.

He stepped to the window in time to see the men put the roll of carpet into the van and drive off. He dressed quickly, packed his toilet articles into his carry-on bag and slipped out the door and down the hall, past the elevator to the stairs. He wasn't sure about checking out but decided against it for he vaguely remembered the chief handing over money when they had entered the hotel. If he had not paid up front, his assailants had probably checked him out to allay any suspicion, since his body was supposed to be removed with no trace.

Leaving the hotel by a side entrance next to the stairs Clay flagged down a taxi, a small Fiat, and by repeating El Alto, El Alto Airport several times he made the driver understand where he wanted to go.

Arriving at the commercial air terminal much earlier than the 1100 hours the Chief had told him to be there, Clay entered the small restaurant and ordered breakfast.

The smell of frying onions permeated the place and after the pisgah sours the night before Clay almost changed his mind about breakfast, but stuck it out.

Most of the people around him were Indios. They had broad faces and were heavy in the chest. More than fifty percent of the population of Bolivia are Indios, however, so it was not strange to see them, especially in the menial jobs.

After he finished his breakfast he walked back to the terminal area.

Clay was jumpy and to his thinking he had a right to be. When people want to kill you it's best to be a little edgy. He mentally cataloged every person he saw, especially the non-Indios, but knew the agency people would not be walking around with a big name tag marked CIA.

He casually walked past the un-manned barrier out onto the tarmac apron and saw a USAF C-130 taking on fuel about a hundred yards away.

He studied the aircraft and crew standing off a safe distance from the plane in case of a fire. Two of the crewmen had big fire extinguishers.

When the refueling was complete one of the airmen placed his extinguisher inside the aircraft then came out and walked quickly toward Clay. That he was coming particularly to speak to Clay there was no doubt, so John Henry walked toward him.

The man said, hesitantly, "Major Clay?"

John Henry answered, "That's right, but it's just John Henry now."

The airman said, "I'm Saul. The chief said to look for a man who walked like he owned the world and would ride tigers. We're to give you a ride to Panama but we need to get you into a set of coveralls, and all I have is this old flight suit," and he pulled the coveralls from his bulging side pocket.

"Did you hear about the chief's accident?"

"No," he said anxiously. "What happened?"

"The chief was killed this morning in a freak accident. The tail gate hatch released suddenly and fell on him and crushed him. The police came and ruled it an accident and released the body to be flown out with the agency's C-130, about an hour ago." The man's eyes filled with tears. Clay could tell by his pain that he and the chief had been good friends.

Clay felt a stillness come over him. He was suddenly in a slow-motion mode. "Do you know where the chief was based, Saul?"

"Yeah, home base was Panama, but it's not a big secret they did a lot of shuttle flying into Nicaragua and Bogota, Columbia."

"How about the agency here? Do they have a permanent station man here?"

"Yeah, the agency man here in Bolivia is the military attache. He's the station chief. No one knows how many agents he has in other embassy slots.

"I see. Thanks for the offer of a ride to Panama but I think I'll decline for now. I want to talk to the agency man before I leave because the chief told me last night something might happen to him." Clay shook hands with the airman and turned and walked away.

His rage and anger were riding him hard but as usual at such time he began talking to himself. What was strange this time was that the voice in his head doing the talking and telling him to "calm down, be cool! take it easy," was the chief's voice.

He found a taxi, another Fiat, and told the driver American Embassy. During the ride to La Paz Clay looked out the windows at the shanties and squalid slums. He had read somewhere that the per capita income in Bolivia was only one hundred twenty dollars per year. The income of the wealthy elite was factored in, meaning thousands of Indians subsisted on virtually nothing except what they could trade and barter.

Another interesting fact, Clay recalled, was that the life expectancy of the average Bolivian was twenty-eight to thirty years. He also remembered hearing the Bolivian Army was about seventy percent Indian and fifty percent illiterate, and the privates were paid two dollars per month. He wondered what their morale must be.

The taxi pulled up to a villa almost entirely covered with ivy. A sign read American Embassy. A single U.S. Marine stood guard at a small drive-through gate. Clay got out of the taxi and paid the driver. Since the Embassy was tucked away in an obviously well-to-do residential area he told the taxi driver to wait but he didn't know whether the man understood him or not.

Pulling his passport out he approached the Marine guard, who didn't even look at it but waved him in.

Entering a large reception area he was met by a slender woman who spoke excellent English with only a slight accent. He asked to see the military attache and was directed down an empty hall to the end office. He entered the wide open door of the end office, and there sat a uniformed lieutenant colonel with crossed cannons insignia, indicating artillery. The insignia could mean a real artillery officer working for the CIA, or a CIA man posing as an artillery officer.

Clay closed the office door behind him and said, "Sir, I want the details of Tommy Thompsons death. Who killed him? Was it the agency or drug smugglers?"

The colonel said, "I don't know what you're talking about and I don't like your attitude. Get out of my office."

Despite the chief's voice in his head saying, "stay cool," John Henry's rage boiled up. He stepped around the desk and suddenly the little pistol with its large silencer was out and pointed at the colonel. Clay pulled the man's head by the hair and placed the muzzle of the pistol against his temple.

"I'll ask you again," he snarled. What happened to the chief?"

The heavy smell of alcohol wafted up from the man although it was still over two hours until noon. He stuttered a denial. John Henry pulled his head back again. "Tell me, you drunken sot, or I'll kill you right now."

Anger made his voice harsh and clipped and for the first time the man sensed he might be in a lot of trouble. He said, "Panama said terminate him with extreme prejudice. I had no choice. But I understand he was drugged and unconscious when they dropped the tail gate on him. He did not suffer."

"Who did the actual killing, man? Quick before I lose control."

An agency man and two of our people from the cartel. I don't know their names. The agency man goes by the name of the Striker and he's usually in Panama or Nicaragua."

John Henry sighed with pain. "Didn't you tell them in Panama he was a no-risk? Didn't you plead for his life? Tell me!"

The CIA colonel, regaining some of his composure and almost sure he wasn't going to be killed, said, "He blabbed to you, and we can't have blabber-mouths in the agency."

John Henry placed the pistol next to the man's temple and almost gently pulled the trigger. The cough of the weapon was even quieter than the sound of the man's head falling on the top of the desk. He reached down and grabbed the man's right hand, slipped the forefinger through the trigger guard, closed his hand around the hand grip and lay the arm, hand and pistol on the desk next to his head with the hole in the temple. A slight trickle of blood oozed out.

Clay felt for a pulse. There was none. He pulled a handkerchief out and wiped all the places he had touched, then moved to the door. He stopped a moment then came back and, using the handkerchief, pulled the left hand drawer open. An almost half full bourbon bottle lay inside. He picked it up by the neck with his handkerchief and, using his teeth, twisted the cap off and set it down on the desk. Then he tipped it over with the nail of his forefinger. The liquor gurgled as the bottle emptied onto the desk.

The scene was perfect for a despondent alcoholic who couldn't take it anymore. He backed out of the office and closed the door with his handkerchief-covered right hand.

He left the embassy and walked through the gate with only a casual wave from the Marine guard, to find his taxi waiting. He got in and said El Alto.

John Henry's dark rage was not softened by the death of the drunken lieutenant colonel. The man's arrogance, smugness and complete lack of remorse at ordering the chief's death had sealed his own fate.

Clay was by profession a killer, a member, or former member, of an elite group whose every waking moment was practicing and training to kill for the U.S. Army—the Green Berets.

This group of well-trained professionals has no real peers anywhere in the free world. To those who are in positions to evaluate these professionals, John Henry was known as the consummate member of this elite group. His proficiency in combat, armed and unarmed, was legend.

The fact that the chief's killers were fellow Americans made no difference to Clay. He had served under the agency and had been around them long enough to know they had no honor.

SIX

Society exists for the benefit, of its members, not the
members for the benefit of society.
Herbert Spencer, Sec. 222
Principles of Ethics

The first thing Clay saw entering the airport terminal was Saul standing near the boarding gate where he could see the aircraft on the tarmac. The terminal was almost deserted. He walked over and Saul greeted him with, "We got delayed for two hours so if you've finished your business you can still ride with us to Howard."

He was referring to Howard Air Force Base in Panama. Clay had been there many times and had stayed there once when he was taking the jungle warfare course, a course which was mostly how to survive in the jungle, not warfare.

"Yes, I've done all I can do here, Saul. Do you still have that old flight suit?"

"Sure, it's right here," and he started tugging and pulling the suit from his lower right leg pocket.

Clay walked to a secluded corner and pulled the no-mex flight suit over his civilian clothes. Then he put one of his two pistols in the roomy side pocket leaving the other one buried deep in his carry-on bag.

Returning to Saul, Clay asked what had delayed their departure. The official reason was a half dozen buss fuses had gone out all at once and there were not enough on hand, but Saul said, "I think the real reason was the aircraft commander had a few too many pisgah sours last night and had to sit on the stool too long."

Clay laughed and asked when they expected to leave. Saul said with some little satisfaction, Clay thought, "The AC's shit out everything but his eyeballs so it should be soon."

Clay asked about boarding and Saul told him anytime, so Clay, begging the same "ailment" as the AC, asked if he could board. Saul walked him to the aircraft and Clay got on and found the pilot, navigator and the other enlisted man already on board.

They were drinking coffee and offered Clay some but he refused and went to the sideboard where there several canvas jump seats were already down. He let down two more and stretched out on them, wondering just how many hours he had spent on just such seats in all types of aircraft during the sixteen years he'd served. So many Clay felt right at home and dozed off.

Saul entered the aircraft and told Clay the AC, a major flying out of England Air Force Base in Louisiana, was amending his flight plan to cover the delay.

Clay sat up and on a hunch said, "Saul, did the chief have an apartment or did he live at the base?"

"The chief had a real nice civilian house, and did he ever throw some parties! He knew most of the American school teachers on contract to the Canal Zone Authority and some of his daiquiri parties are still talked about!"

"Do you have his address?"

"Sure," Saul said, "I'll write it down for you cause it's got a bunch of numbers. I mainly just know how to get there on Friday and Saturday nights. You know what I mean?"

"Yeah, I've been to some of the chief's parties!" He and Saul laughed although both felt like crying.

The chief's address was on Balboa Street in Panama City and there must have been ten numbers in the address.

The air force major finally entered the aircraft and stepped up the two steps onto the flight deck. Soon the props were turning and shortly after that they took off.

An hour later they landed at Howard AFB, Panama.

John Henry grabbed a civilian taxi that had just off-loaded some military people, probably shipping out or going on leave to the states.

He showed the address to the taxi driver who made a u-turn and drove right through the gate despite a sign that said in both English and Spanish, Stop for Air Police. Clay thought fondly, my kind of cabbie.

After considerable twisting and turning through many narrow streets the cabbie pulled up at a house on a short block of four or five houses and pointed to the second house on the right. But Clay wasn't paying attention. Instead he was watching what looked like a military style sedan pull around the far corner and out of sight.

Of course there were other houses on the brick street, but Clay had a feeling he had just missed the agency's control team checking the chief's house.

SEVEN

Carrying his carry-on bag and still in Saul's nomex
flight suit, Clay walked up the twisting but short walk
through flowering vines and ferns.

The front door was ajar. Clay set his bag down and
drew the .32 caliber pistol with attached silencer from his
leg pocket and, using the barrel of his weapon, pushed the
door open and walked in.

The living room looked like a war-zone. The spacious
living room with glass French doors leading to an enclosed
patio had obviously been ransacked. Furniture was overturned, pictures pulled off the walls and cushions slit open
and stuffing pulled out.

Pistol held out in front of him Clay walked to the bedroom. It was also torn up. Stuffing from the cut open mattress was everywhere. A small wall safe hung open. The
rest of the house was the same. Whoever had searched the
place had been very thorough.

He returned to the front door and collected his bag,
re-entered the house and shut the door. Clay knew that

amateurs were sometimes more successful than professionals. He would stay here and put the chief's place back together and maybe in the process find out about the agency man, the Striker, who had killed him. Besides, Clay knew the chief as well as anyone and he was positive that somewhere, somehow, he would have iron-clad proof of what the agency was doing. He was that kind of man.

The smell of liquor led Clay back to the kitchen, which was a mess like the remainder of the house. The searchers had overturned the chief's liquor cabinet and at least half of the fifteen or twenty bottles of booze lay broken on the tile floor. Clay found an unbroken bottle of Puerto Rico Light Rum and proceeded to open it and gulp down a large swig.

Setting the table back on its legs and righting the chairs Clay sat down and thought about what he was going to do.

One thing was definitely in his favor: the agency knew nothing about him or his background. They did not know he had operated behind enemy lines, and made snatch operations—going into enemy compounds to capture and remove prisoners for interrogation. He had also fought in ferocious ground battles and lived the horrors of war as few other men had. The truth was, he was uniquely qualified to search out and terminate the people who had killed his friend.

First, he would find proof of the agency's involvement in drug smuggling. He was sure that the chief had documented it somehow and hidden the proof.

Second, he would find the CIA agent known as the Striker, and kill him for the murder of the chief.

With no more of a plan than that Clay began the cleanup—and search—of the chief's house. By ten o'clock the house was in fairly decent order but Clay had found absolutely nothing, not even a clue, as to where the chief might have hidden any information. Worse, there appeared to be no food anywhere in the house. He had found a set of car keys for a Ford Motor Company auto, but the small carport at the back of the house was empty.

Recalling some photos torn from their frames and stewn around the bedroom, he remembered a photo of the chief standing beside a small car. He hurried to the bedroom and rifled through the eight or ten photos he had laid on top of the chest of drawers while cleaning up.

He found a shot of the chief beside a blue and white English Ford. The photo was a recent one and Clay knew he had transportation if he could find the car. Also, the information he was searching for could be hidden in the Ford.

Thinking it through Clay realized the car was probably close to the agency's flight hanger, which he figured was also at Howard AFB and more than likely near the main terminal where he had off-loaded early that afternoon.

He had not eaten since early in the morning in La Paz, Bolivia and was starving so he locked the doors and headed for a lighted area several blocks away.

There he found an American–style fast food emporium and ate three large, greasy cheeseburgers with french fries and felt as though he might live.

Deciding not to wait until the next day, Clay donned the flight suit again and caught a taxi. At the gate the air policeman caught a glimpse of the flight suit and waved the cabbie on in.

He settled with the taxi driver and got out at the main terminal and started walking through the parking lots. Just before midnight, after forty-five minutes of walking and searching, Clay found it. He compared it to the one in the photo then tried the key. It worked. Clay got in and started it up, and after a few minutes of some rough idling it smoothed out and Clay pulled out of the lot and headed for the main gate.

He turned his lights off so the gate guard could see the blue decal on the left front bumper and was waved through. Clay returned to the Chief's house.

He decided to wait until morning to search the car except for a quick look in the glove compartment and in the rear seat. He locked it up and went inside to get some sleep.

The mattress was plush, although a little lumpy where Clay had stuffed the loose stuffing back into it, and placing one of his pistols on the pillow next to him Clay quickly dropped off to sleep.

EIGHT

*"War is Hideous! and yet—I feel sorry, neither for
the friend nor for the friend's mother, but for those
who have never been to war."*

Anon

At two thirty AM Clay was awakened by a small noise.
He grabbed his pistol and rolled to the side of the bed,
pointed the loaded .32 at the bedroom door and waited.

A few moments later he heard another small sound
coming from outside.

He got up, slipped on the flight suit and tip-toed to
the rear side door. Two men with flashlights were system-
atically taking the car apart.

He had decided there were only two when he saw the
flare of a lighted cigarette as a third man, apparently the
guard, took a deep drag.

During his sixteen years of army time Clay had spent
numerous hours stalking sentries, most not as careless as
this one. He considered his options and decided to go
outside.

Mentally marking where the guard had placed himself
Clay backed away from that door and tip-toed to the front
part of the house.

John Henry had noted the strange awe American soldiers had for the enemy, often attributing to them almost supernatural powers to operate in the dark and in complete silence. He himself had found for the most part they were not nearly as well trained nor as efficient in night movement as Americans.

John Henry knew he was one of the best at using the night and darkness to his advantage. In Vietnam he had on several occasions reconned in front of their perimeters and caught the famed Viet Cong Sappers infiltrating American positions.

One time using his knife he had killed four. When the remaining two could not feel nor hear the others, they quickly withdrew while Clay was still stalking them.

Clay tip-toed into the kitchen and by feel selected a butcher knife with an eight inch blade. He tested the edge with his thumb. It was razor sharp.

Putting his pistol in his roomy leg pocket Clay padded to the front door, unlocked it and eased it open. No one was watching the front of the house. Moving like a shadow John Henry slipped through the door and entered the verdant overgrown sideyard.

He waited for some ten minutes and, hearing nothing, began to stalk the guard near the carport.

John Henry felt no hesitation about what he was preparing to do. These men, American or Hispanic, CIA or cartel, had killed his friend. They were the enemy in this war. Was it his fault the bastards had sent second team people against him?

There are people in the forces who would have told them Clay was first team in every sense of the phrase. If they had not been told they were in a war, and up against a professional, it was no fault of his. He knew the Striker was not in the group he was after, so except for the one he needed to interrogate, the rest were dog meat.

A sense of morality often affects the way men face combat, but John Henry had decided that if the enemy's morality put him into the fray against Americans, he would not hesitate to eliminate them.

The other question was the matter of loyalty. Could he be loyal to a government agency that had killed his friend after he had given over 25 years of loyal service? No.

When the people facing him had killed the chief they had not been concerned with morality. No more reasoning was required of him, regardless of the fact he was now most probably facing Americans.

Slipping through the heavy foliage Clay stepped upon what felt like a brick walkway leading to a back yard and the chief's carport. The walk turned and he smelled the strong, foul odor of a heavy cigarette smoker around the corner from him.

Clay brought the knife up to a few inches above his belt line and stepped around the corner.

The guard was there. Clay covered his mouth and at the same time plunged his knife into him—in and up, twisting and turning it to reach vital organs.

The guard slumped. Clay held him up a few seconds then almost gently let him fall to the walkway.

He wiped his knife on the man's shirt then placed it on a nearby flower pot.

He pulled out his pistol and walked the half dozen steps to where the two men were searching the car. All the while the chief's voice whispered in his head, Careful, John Henry.

He leaned in with the pistol in front of him and said, "Found anything yet?"

One of them said, "Nothing yet. Then suddenly realizing the voice was strange went for his pistol hung under his left arm pit in a shoulder rig.

He was fast and almost had the weapon out when Clay's .32 coughed and a hole appeared in his forehead. He fell to the ground. The other man froze.

Clay said, "Son, you're in a lot of trouble. Do you want to live?"

"Yes, sir. I'll cooperate."

"Good, then without touching the flashlight nor that pistol your partner pulled I want you to show me where your weapon is."

The man slowly eased back his jacket lapel revealing a shoulder rig.

Clay told him to lean forward. When the man complied he reached over and pulled the CIA .32 out.

"Now, Clay said, "pick up the closest flashlight and we'll walk around the house and go inside."

The man did as he was told just glancing briefly at the body of the guard as they moved to the front of the house.

Clay flipped on the lights and shut the door. Then he looked at his prisoner.

The man was older than he had appeared in the light of the flash lights and had agency written all over him.

"You people killed a friend of mine for no reason. I intend to find the man who did it and anyone who gets in my way will be dealt with harshly. Now, what are you looking for?"

The man said almost matter of factly, "You don't know who you're dealing with. We're the CIA, Americans just like you . . ."

Clay stopped him. "Hold on. I don't want any of your bull-shit. I worked for the agency myself and I know what bastards most of you are." You've got one slim chance to live and not be thrown into the canal with your dead buddies outside."

The man's face tensed up a little and he had a movement in his right eye, almost a tic. "You know you'll be hunted down and killed for this, don't you?"

"First of all, asshole, I'm not your everyday tourist down here. Uncle Sam used to refer to us as Paid Professional Killers in Green Berets. Well, I will bring it to you guys as long as I can and until I catch up with the fun-and-games guy that killed the chief. Now, I'll ask again, what were you looking for?"

The man's right eye was really jumping now and the white shirt under the tan suit jacket he wore was wet with sweat. He had bright eyes and bushy eyebrows that almost met. He appeared to be extremely nervous.

"Big Hand thought Thompson might have kept a log of everything the agency has done including names of the cartel members we've worked with."

"Who is Big Hand?" Clay asked leaning forward, his penetrating eyes boring holes in his prisoner.

"The DIC, Director in Charge, of Operation Big Hand. I think he operates from Miami."

This man was frightened. He had looked at his watch three times since they had entered the house. Long years of facing danger had heightened Clay's senses and the feeling of impending action or disaster was with him now.

He looked at his own watch; it was 02:45. Clay decided to play a hunch. "I think you're telling me the truth so I'm going to tie you up, then at six o'clock we'll take your buddies for a drive along the canal and throw them in."

The man began to beg. "Please let me go. I won't say a thing about all this."

"Can't do that. You've got to help me put the car back together in the morning."

He said, almost hysterically, A fire-bomb is set to go off at five thirty. We've got to get out of here."

"Where is it?"

"Against the back wall of the house. It's on a timer and it's set in 25 pounds of C-4 plastic explosion."

"Then we'd better go disarm it."

The frightened man told Clay the timer was very sensitive, exactly for that very reason: in case someone discovered it and tried to dismantle it.

Clay had spent many years using explosives and he thought he knew the timer the man was referring to. They were, indeed, very tricky. But if they had used C-4 maybe it was in two-pound blocks and he could remove them all leaving the timing device with no more power than a M-80 fire cracker. It was worth a check.

They went out the rear door and the man led him to a package about the size of a small suitcase.

Clay didn't want to turn on the outside lights because of the two bodies lying there in plain sight, so he handed the flashlight to the CIA man and told him to hold it steady; one mistake and both of them would be dead meat.

The man shivered and stammered, "Don't worry, I'll be good."

John Henry carefully opened the package. There were twelve blocks of C-4. The timer had been wedged between two of them.

After he took the last block out Clay ordered the man to stack the now harmless C-4 in the trunk of the car. He also had him pile the two bodies into it and he held the pistol on the man while he recovered the pistols dropped by the dead man. A pistol-grip 12-gauge riot gun also lay on the ground. Evidently the men had recovered it from the chief's car. Clay took it. Then he had the man put the seats back into the car and he held the gun on him while he used a battery pack screw-driver to put the door panels back on. He also had him put all the bits and pieces that remained into the back seat.

Leaving the one back door of the Ford open Clay had the man pick up the box with the timer in it and set it down in the back seat. Then Clay ordered the man into the driver's seat and pitched him the keys.

"You drive. Go north until we can get close to the canal."

"Yes, sir." Then he asked, "What are you going to do with me?"

"You present a problem, Amigo. By rights I ought to kill you, but I did say I wouldn't if you cooperated. On the other hand, if I turn you loose you'll be on the phone in ten minutes to the agency."

"No sir. I'm out of it. The agency don't pay me enough. I've never liked this Operation Big Hand anyway. They said when it started the blacks would get their drugs anyway and if we hauled it in to them we'd get money to help the Contras against the Sandinistas. But, those people are Americans and I'm real uncomfortable with what we've been doing."

"OK, so what's your name?"

"Jessie Taylor, and I'm from Lakeland, Florida. When you turn me loose that's where I'm heading."

"Jessie, let me tell you something. The agency is in the wrong big-time and I'm going to make some people pay. If I run into you again in this fight you're dog meat. Understand?"

"Yes, sir, but I need to warn you. The Striker is bad news and he's second in command to Big Hand. He does a lot of the dirty work because he purely does love it."

"Do you know where he is now?"

"All we've heard is he's in the boonies of Nicaragua organizing and recruiting for the Contras."

Soon they came to a stretch of the road to Colon that swung close to the canal. Only a two-strand barbed wire fence protected it.

The Canal Zone is a five-mile wide, fifty–mile long strip of land running from Colon on the Atlantic side to Panama City on the Pacific side. It's controlled by the Canal Zone Authority, but they have no military forces nor is there a need for any.

Clay stopped the car on a narrow stretch where the two-strand barbed wire fence was close to the road. They each dragged a body under the fence and then to the canal. Then they pushed them over the side and listened for the two splashes as they hit the water. Returning to the car they carefully unloaded the box with the timer still in it, ticking away, and left it under a culvert, out of sight of the road.

Clay turned around and sped off toward Panama City. It was exactly 04:30.

John Henry was going to drop his prisoner at a taxi stand in the city but Jessie told him the agency had a car parked close to the chief's house. When Clay dropped him off, he saw it was the same car he had spotted leaving the prior evening.

Clay gave the man one more warning. "Stay out of this and you'll live a lot longer."

"Yes sir. You won't see me again."

NINE

"Never forget, your weapon was made by the lowest bidder."
Rule 7, Murphy's Law of Combat

Clay headed to a commercial area and found an early morning restaurant. Having been up for about four hours Clay was ready for some coffee and maybe some breakfast while he did some thinking.

As he sipped his coffee he considered what he had. The agency had not found anything in the chief's house or his car. Clay had meant to double check but now he had to assume the log or documents were not there. The chief probably had a locker at the air terminal, but Clay knew the agency would look there first. Therefore, they were somewhere else.

In all the time John Henry had known the chief he always had a woman stashed somewhere close at hand. Would he have had a girl here in Panama? Yes. But would it have been one of the beautiful hispanic girls Panama was loaded with? Or would it be one of the American school teachers Saul had talked about always being at the chief's parties.

Clay knew the chief had been a great admirer of thin, nubile, dark haired girls and was forever chasing them. But

Clay also knew there had been no "round eyes" in Vietnam, perhaps his desires were based on availability, not just young and skinny only.

The waitress brought him his *huevo-tocino* omelet and Clay left off his heavy thinking to get around a good, well cooked breakfast.

Finishing his food Clay thought, where would one find an American school teacher? And immediately he answered himself. At the Canal Zone American school.

While paying for his meal he casually asked the English–speaking cashier where the school was located. She gave him directions to the Canal Zone dependent housing section not too far off, and said the housing section circled the school so he would have no problem finding it.

He thanked her and left just as the sun peeped over the horizon. He got into the chief's car and headed in the direction given him, although, he thought, school wouldn't be open until at least 8:00 o: clock and the teachers probably wouldn't start arriving until 7:00 or 7:30 and it was just now 0600 hours. Nevertheless he drove there and found the school, a white stucco, two-story structure with a red terra–cotta roof, and parked across the street.

Several times he almost drifted off to sleep and once he got out and walked around the car to stretch his legs. Eight o'clock came and went and Clay knew the school wasn't going to open. He thought back and finally worked it out; it was Saturday.

He turned on the motor when a car pulled into the school's front parking lot. A young woman, dressed casually and very pretty by any standard, got out and started for the entrance.

Clay got to the entrance at the same time as the young lady.

She looked up inquiringly. "Yes?"

55

"Excuse me, but are you a teacher here?"

"Yes I am. I'm just here to pick up some term papers. If you have business with the school you'll have to see the superintendent on Monday."

"No, I don't have business with the school. I'm looking for a lady who's a good friend of Tommy Thompson. I understand he is friends with a school teacher working for the Canal Zone Authority."

"You must mean Karen. She's his fiancee and they're planning to get married soon."

"Well, I've got real bad news for Karen. I need to talk to her personally. Could you tell me where she lives?"

"Oh God, I hope nothing's happened to the Chief. She lives and breathes for him."

"I'm afraid I've got bad news. He's been killed. Could you come with me to break it to her?"

"Oh hell! She finally fell in love and now this. Yeah, I'll get the papers I came here for and you can follow me to her place. Dammit to hell!"

A few minutes later she pulled out of the parking lot and headed east. The drive took only ten minutes.

As they pulled up to the house two men came down the short walk, half dragging a petite, dark haired young woman in her late twenties. The teacher Clay was following jumped out of her car and started screaming at the two men pulling the girl.

It was a distraction enough that the two men failed to notice Clay's hasty stop. He jumped out of his car and lined up the sights of the CIA's .32 caliber pistol on the first man, but quickly shifted to the second man when he pulled out his pistol and aimed it at the teacher who had led him here.

Clay's pistol coughed. The man stopped sideways and his pistol fired up at the sky. Clay could barely hear it. The CIA did go in for silencers, thank goodness.

56

The first man holding on to the young woman was shocked to see his partner lying on the ground with a hole in the right side of his head. But he recovered quickly, shoved the young woman down and pulled out his own .32. Clay shot him right in the center of his forehead. He fell backwards across the body of his partner.

The young woman lying on the ground quickly got up and ran to her friend. They stood there holding one another, the chief's girl friend sobbing loudly.

Clay looked around. It seemed as though the neighborhood was still sleeping. He put his pistol away and quickly picked up the two bodies and put them in their military style sedan. He also stashed both pistols in the rear of their car.

He went to the women and urged them inside the house. Then he introduced himself as John Henry, an old friend of the chief. The young woman he had identified as the chief's fiancee, Karen, said, "You're the John Henry Clay the chief's always talking about?" and with that she cried out, "Please tell me it's not so. The chief can't be dead! No! No!"

"He was murdered in La Paz by one of his own people, the one they call the Striker, and I'm trying to find him."

"The chief was always talking about a really mean bastard called the Striker. I believe he said his name was Holliman, Holiman, Holman, or something like that."

"What about those two men who were trying to take you off? Do you know who they were?"

"They said the chief was dead and they were taking me in for questioning. They had badges, but they didn't act like policemen."

"Karen, it's very important for me to find any papers or other items the chief hid away just in case something like this happened. Do you know anything about them?"

"No, the chief never gave me anything to hold, but wait—he did once tell me if anything ever happened to him he had an old friend from Vietnam who knew about his personal papers, his will and other things. In fact, he wrote his friend's name and address on a card and I have it here somewhere." She got up and with the other woman trailing after her, went down a little hall to a bedroom.

The small house had pretty modern furniture and vases with flowers and flower pots with blooming flowers were everywhere.

There were ash trays but they were spotlessly clean so Clay knew she kept them there only for the chief.

The fragrance of jasmine filled the house but Clay couldn't tell if it was perfume or from the blooming plants.

Karen returned with a 3 by 5 card. "Here it is. The man's name is Robert Whipple. He was in Special Forces in Vietnam. The chief said you and Whipple were very much alike, no-nonsense, professional soldiers who would fight till the end for what you believed in. Do you think he might know something?"

"Whipple's name is very familiar, but it doesn't bring up a face. He's in Costa Rica so that'll be my next stop."

"I'm going too because the chief told me some things we might have to tell Whipple to get his cooperation."

"No way, Karen. These people are playing for keeps and I don't want to have to worry about you if I meet more of them."

"But I can't stay here. They'll be back to get me."

"Damn," Clay said, "You're right. Those bastards will be back. Alright, we'll go together and after we talk to Whipple we'll make other arrangements."

"No, I want to see you kill the bastard that murdered the Chief."

58

"Wait Karen, are you sure about this?" her girl friend asked.

"Yes, Mary Beth, my life is over now. All I want is to get somebody for what they did. I've paid my bills and the rent so there's no reason to stay. In my frame of mind I couldn't teach anyway. Would you explain for me?"

"Of course." Fifteen minutes later Karen hugged Mary Beth goodbye and got into the chief's car. She would follow Clay while he drove the agency vehicle.

He stopped the car in a remote spot northwest of town, wiped it for fingerprints, took out the pistols and all their ammo and he joined Karen in the chief's car. After gassing up and checking the oil and tires, Clay got behind the wheel and they set out on the Inter-American highway for Bogua-teo, Panama, some 225 miles away.

There they would cross into Costa Rica, then head to San Jose, the capital, another 125 miles away. Karen had traveled to San Jose several times so she was familiar with the trip.

That night they were somewhere in southern Costa Rica. There appeared to be no motels, but they stopped for some directions and Karen used her excellent Spanish to find a place that took overnight guests. Having been on the road for nine hours and with less than two hours sleep the night before, Clay was ready to crash.

TEN

If all mankind minus one, were of one opinion, and only one person were of the contrary opinion, mankind would be no more justified in silencing that one person, than he, if he had the power, would be justified in silencing mankind.
John Stuart Mill (Liberty, Ch 2)

The CIA deputy director of operations had the director of Big Hand (and he wondered just who in hell he was) on a conference phone call. No pleasantries were exchanged.

"Just what the hell is going on down there?" the deputy director asked. "We've got a station chief who's blown himself away; we've got four agents killed in line of duty; we have an agent missing, presumed dead, and one of our contract aviators was killed in a freak accident. And all in one week."

"Sir, we have a paranoid killer loose in Panama who has a hard-on for the agency. I'm taking steps to have him apprehended to stand trial for murder."

"Negative, Big Hand. No trials. Take care of this man immediately. What about that contract killer you have on the payroll down there, the Striker? Can't you put him onto this ass-hole?"

"Yes sir. He's coming back to Panama to take care of it."

"Good! Now, do you need any replacement personnel for your operation?"

"No sir, not at the present time. We can continue with the people we have."

The deputy director hung up, still wondering what Operation Big Hand was all about and why regular reports weren't being sent to Ops.

In Miami Big Hand was already calling Panama to instruct the Striker to find that damn maverick friend of the chief before he did any more damage. He knew he was very short-handed but he also knew he couldn't take a chance on any new personnel because some bleeding heart might blow the whistle on the entire operation. They would just have to make do.

ELEVEN

"War has no fury like a non-combatant."
Charles Montague (Disenchantment)

The next morning Karen and Clay were on the Inter-American. The macadam highway wove through the jungle, and at some points the vines and flowering shrubs were threatening to cover the road. They passed through small villages, most with the pleasing aroma of cooking food, beans and other vegetables and smiling, waving people.

Some forty miles south of San Jose they passed a road crew patching the pavement and cutting the jungle growth back from the road. John Henry figured it was a permanent and continuous job.

Along one long, lonely stretch of the highway Clay stopped the car and, taking one of their captured .32 caliber pistols, had Karen shoot at a man-sized tree trunk from fifty feet. He was pleasantly surprised when she hit the tree dead center four of the five shots she took. Clay simply said, "The chief?" She nodded and said he'd taught her to use a pistol, rifle, and even a shotgun with a pistol grip.

Clay pointed to the trunk of the car and told her the Chief's pistol grip, 12-gauge shotgun was there. She again nodded, big tears in her eyes.

Karen had a small boned petite figure and long black hair with startling blue eyes. When she talked about the chief the tears would come and twice she'd made Clay promise that if the opportunity presented itself she would kill the chief's murderer.

They came into the outskirts of San Jose, a modern, clean city with friendly people. Following the road signs they were able to circumvent most of the city as they headed toward Punfarenas, Costa Rica. Clay wondered why Bob Whipple lived there. He was probably too young to be retired, although a lot of Americans were moving to Costa Rica because of its great climate, low cost of living and stable, friendly government.

Whipple lived in Punfarenas, on the Pacific coast, or at least on the Gulf of Nicoya. The town had a population of about 30,000. From what Clay had heard there was a sizable American colony there made up of retirees and disaffected Americans.

Clay pulled in to a quaint roadside restaurant on the western outskirts of San Jose and they ate a fairly late lunch.

As he talked to Karen, John Henry found himself telling her not only about his exploits with the chief but also more and more about himself. And as he talked he felt a lot of bitterness wash away and evaporate. As they enjoyed a cup of coffee after their meal, Clay glanced idly through the window and saw a blue sedan speed by. It had an oversized USA license tag and looked like the cars bought and issued to the U.S. military. The back of Clay's neck tingled. He knew his hunch was right because a few minutes later the car returned and cruised through the parking lot, slowing down when it passed the chief's blue and white English Ford. Then they got back on the highway and sped west.

It wasn't hard to figure out that the people in the car were CIA and that they were on their way to Bob Whipple's. Clay knew they'd never catch up with the big sedan and wondered how to get word on ahead to Whipple.

Luckily the restaurant had a public telephone. After he agreed to pay the charges, the proprietors got Senor Robert Whipple on the line. A moment later Clay heard a deep male voice with a faint trace of a Georgia accent. "This is Robert Whipple, who's calling please?"

Clay answered quickly. "Bob, this is John Henry Clay, a good friend of the chiefs. He's been killed and I have reason to believe some of the people involved in his death are on their way to see you right now."

"What? Did you say the chief has been killed?"

"Roger that, Bob. The Chief's girl friend and I are in San Jose right now. We were on our way to see you when several men passed us when we stopped to eat. They're bad news, fellow, and I have a feeling they'll want to get whatever the chief left with you, and then kill you. Take steps to protect himself and we'll get there as quick as we can."

"Okay. Put Karen on the line."

Clay handed Karen the phone. She spoke to Whipple for a few moments and then wordlessly handing the phone back to Clay, and turned and walked to the big picture window, tears streaming down her face.

Clay said, "John Henry here."

"I had to ask Karen some raw questions so she's probably upset, but I had to know for sure it was her. "I'll button down the hatches for a siege but if these guys are any good, I won't be able to hold them off too long. I've got a cook here who doesn't know one end of a gun from another, and a young man who works the gardens for me, and his expertise with a weapon is about the same as the cook's.

"I'm wheel-chair bound from stepping on a land mine in Vietnam so I can't move around enough to hold off a determined attack."

"Do your best, Bob. We're on our way in the chief's car."

Whipple gave some quick directions to his villa from the Inter-American highway and Clay hung up the phone. He paid the food and phone bills and they went to the car. Clay thought a few seconds, then opened the trunk and took out the pistol-grip shotgun and twelve shells.

In the car Clay instructed Karen on how to hold the weapon so she could shoot quickly in case they were way-laid on the way.

They had to drive fifty miles and with the road being as good as it appeared to be thought they would make it in about an hour.

Fifty five minutes later they were looking for a paved lane. The lush jungle was so thick they almost missed it, and Clay wasn't surprised to see the sedan he'd spotted at the restaurant some fifty yards in.

It was empty. Tracks showed it and had been pulled off to one side, then backed into a small space so they could drive off quickly. There was no key in the ignition and the trunk stood open. They had obviously removed weapons.

Clay considered Karen. She saw it and shook her head. "No, John Henry. I'm in this all the way."

"All right but I lead and if I start shooting you fade to one side or another and only shoot to kill when you get a clear shot."

When finished he thought of just how ridiculous it was to tell someone armed with a shot gun to "shoot to kill."

Clay led off at a good speed and soon saw a beautiful wood-frame home with a verandah style porch running completely across the front.

Using huge bougainvillea bushes as cover they managed to get to within five or six steps of the porch without showing themselves, when suddenly they heard a loud blast from a twelve-gauge shotgun, and the answering stacato hammering of a sub-machine gun.

Three men came rushing out onto the porch, obviously trying to escape the deadly shotgun.

None fit the description he had of the Striker, but the fact they were attacking Bob Whipple told Clay they were CIA or hired thugs.

John Henry held a tight sight picture on the chest of the first man out when Karen's shotgun roared, and the man he was sighting on was thrown backwards.

Clay lined up his pistol on the second man. His .32 coughed and the man jerked to a stop, and then toppled to the ground.

The third man hammered a burst from his Uzi and Clay's pistol spoke again, twice in quick succession and the man dropped the little sub-machine gun and grabbed his stomach. He took several steps toward Clay and Karen with a questioning look on his face and as he went down he let out a plaintive scream and the questioning look turned to horror and disbelief.

Clay held the pistol out in front of himself, but believed they had killed all their enemies. He cautiously approached the porch and ascended the steps, stopping at the side of the now open door.

"Bob," he yelled. "This is John Henry Clay. Are you all right?"

"Yeah, we're OK. How about the bad guys?"

"We got three of them. Are there more?"

"No. That's it. Come on in." Clay heard a rolling sound and a moment later saw Bob Whipple in a large motorized wheelchair.

They looked at one another and Clay suddenly went back to a rainy day at Field Forces II Headquarters, and heard Colonel Harrison asking him to say a few words on enemy tactics and techniques to eight new lieutenants just reporting in.

One of the eight had a thousand questions and was not the least bashful about asking them. They were smart, discerning questions and although he was slightly irritated Clay answered them as well as he could.

That lieutenant was now sitting in his big wheelchair with no legs. He chuckled at Clay's start of recognition and said, "Well, John Henry, I guess I'm finally out of questions."

Clay stepped forward and they shook hands, a tight clasp that told each other their mutual appreciation of the other's sacrifices and accomplishments.

"How's it going, buddy?" Whipple knew Clay was not asking about the present but about his terrible loss in a lost war.

"It's not bad. I have periods when I just want to get up and run somewhere, but then I realize I came back. A lot of guys didn't as you well know."

A step sounded and Clay wheeled, crouched and had his pistol out facing a young man who froze seeing this immediate reaction to his appearance.

"No, Clay, he's my gardener!" John Henry straightened and returned the little pistol to his belt.

"Sorry, amigo."

The shaken young man caught his breath and pulled the window drapes aside. The light revealed a large living room with heavy furniture that had a definite Spanish flavor. It was both masculine and comfortable, and it fit Bob Whipple like a glove.

Fifteen or twenty 7MM bullet holes ran along the hall and across a door, which was hanging open with one hinge shot away.

Now Clay looked for Karen.

He moved out on the porch and put his arm around her. "You did good, honey. Don't have any regrets where these killers are concerned."

Clay picked up the pump shotgun and worked the handguard lever. A spent shell flew out and a new one went into the chamber. He put the safety on and turned the gun bottom up and put in another shell. It was again loaded with one in the chamber and four in the magazine. The gun had no plug in it to reduce the magazine capacity as sporting guns had.

Whipple came out on the porch and looked at the three bodies. "That one is agency; the other two are drug cartel."

"What do we do with the bodies, amigo?"

"We'll bury them out back. Juan Miguel will help."

Clay and the young gardener carried the bodies to a clearing behind the house. While the gardener went to the tool house to find shovels and some canvas to wrap them in, John Henry stripped the bodies of their money, a .32 pistol and two 7mm Uzi's. Clay was still financially strapped so taking their money did not bother him in the least.

The agency man had a small notebook with several names and numbers, one with the code name Big Hand and a telephone number with the Miami area code 305. Several towns in Nicaragua were listed and Clay figured there were strong CIA efforts there to recruit and organize people for the Contras.

The young gardener returned with shovels and some canvas to wrap the bodies in. John Henry started digging. They finished the one big grave and together he and the gardener rolled the bodies in the light canvas and placed them in their mutual grave. They ran together in life, let them rot together in the same hole.

It was late afternoon by the time they finished the burial and Karen, Clay and Bob Whipple got together in the big living room for a conference.

It was agreed that Karen should stay behind while Clay carried on the hunt for the chief's murderer in Nicaragua. Karen had had her taste of combat and hadn't liked it much, so she didn't put up a lot of resistance. She was no longer bloodthirsty after her taste of combat.

The two men planned what Clay would have to take: compass, map, rations, weapons and ammo. Whipple could provide almost everything and Clay had the little .32s with silencers, the two Uzi's and the chief's 12 gauge riot gun with the pistol grip.

Bob was also able to give Clay a good run-down on the conflict between the Contras, being sponsored by the U.S., and the Sandinistas who represented the socialist government controlling the country under Daniel Ortega.

TWELVE

*"There are two worlds, the world we can measure
with line and rule, and the world that we feel with
our hearts and imagination."*
Leigh Hunt (Fiction and Matters of Fact.)

Whipple had no papers or documents but he had a
safe deposit box key with a bearer's authorization letter to
a bank in Miami, Florida. He said the chief had told him
to give it to anyone known to be a friend of his who was
not from the agency.

The three of them decided to leave the key with Bob
and Karen who would stay with him while Clay was looking for the chief's killer in Nicaragua. Clay would then
come back and pick up the key.

Whipple briefed Clay and told him the Inter-American
highway, called down there the Pan-American highway,
led right through Nicaragua. He said it was an open border
and although the Sandinistas, under El Presidente, Daniel
Ortega elected in 1984, were everywhere and controlled
most of the country, they allowed almost free movement.

Bob went on, "They're a "leftist movement" but they
don't want to be labeled "Communist" so they have a fa-
cade of freedom." He went on, "After you cross the border

it's about 30 kilometers to the first town, which is Rivas then you go on up along the west side of Lake Nicaragua to Managua, the capital."

Lake Nicaragua was famous because it is the only fresh water body that contains sharks and other salt water fish.

The Sandinistas are named after General Augusto Cesar Sandino, who controlled the country in the early 1900s. In 1933 he was killed by the National Guard that the U.S. had installed before pulling out in 1932.

Bob continued his briefing. "In trying to keep the Communists out of South America the U.S. is backing rebel forces called the Contras, by financing and arming them to fight the Sandinistas. We've got some Special Forces Teams in the country training them, and the CIA has a hands on mission there."

Clay listened, although he had known most of it and guessed a lot more. He recalled from his area-studies of South America that the eastern coastal area was referred to as the Mosquito Coast after the Indians that lived there. The Mosquito coastal area was hot, humid, sparsely populated jungle with an annual rainfall of over 165 inches.

There was a central highlands with well built towns and nice adobe homes. There were several active or live volcanoes and earthquakes were frequent throughout the country.

Two years ago the U.S. had imposed a trade embargo against Nicaragua which had resulted in severe economic problems for the country.

Whipple told Clay he could follow the Pan-American highway through the capital and then to the east to a small town called Sebaco. From Sebaco he could go into the jungle to locate the man directing and organizing the Contras, although he pointed out large Contra groups were running cross border operations from their safe areas in Honduras.

Clay was told and shown where the safety deposit key would be in case something happened to Whipple. The men also planned a defense of the villa should the agency send more men. With Karen and a few lessons in weaponry to Bob's cook and gardener they should be able to hold off anything but a determined attack and siege.

Clay took his captured arms, his carry-on bag, a small ruck-sack and the supplies Bob was providing him to the agency car in preparation for a before daylight departure. Karen was very subdued at the evening meal and later when Clay brought the agency car up to the front of the house she said that although she still wanted the chief avenged, she couldn't stand to see it.

She had agreed to stay with Bob until Clay returned from Nicaragua. She would help defend the villa if the agency sent more people, but killing one man with her shotgun had taken the starch out of her.

John Henry was relieved for he knew that where he was going he'd be hard-pressed to protect them both. He promised her the chief would be avenged, however, and with a quick kiss on the cheek they retired for the night.

The next morning at 0400 hours Clay threw the little ruck-sack with its rations, gun oil, soap, towel, extra ammunition and Whipple's Shell Oil Company road map of Nicaragua, into the agency car and drove off.

The drive to the border in the big, heavy Chevrolet sedan took three hours. After crossing the border Clay saw the Sandinistas everywhere: on bridges, in front of government buildings and generally watching everything taking place. They were dressed in a variety of army field clothes, mostly U.S. Army fatigues, but Clay noted their weapons, mostly Ak-47s and mostly Communist–made, were clean and handled professionally.

When he arrived in Rivas he was getting low on gas so he pulled into a Shell station. He had no problem getting his gas and he checked his oil himself, but no one was friendly and even a two dollar tip only elicited a muttered gracious.

There were signs everywhere. Clay soon realized they were election signs. Daniel Ortega was running to keep his job as the El Presidente of Nicaragua. Unlike some countries in South America having elections, everything seemed to be peaceful.

On the road again Clay noted that the country, while beautiful, was not flourishing as Costa Rica appeared to be. The United States was enforcing the economic embargo on Nicaragua they had started in 1985, claiming that the Sandinista government was, if not communist, very much a leftist regime. This was enough to deaden the overall mien of the population.

Some two hours later Clay was on the east side of Managua, the capital city. He continued following the old Pan–American highway south of Lake Managua, now heading east by slightly northeast. He was planning on going into the Contra–controlled jungle area just northeast of Sebaco. He had a compass and the Shell Oil Company map had contour lines and showed most of the rivers and streams.

At 1500 hours, 3:00 P.M. Clay drove through the little town of Sebaco, then turned off the Pan-American highway when it turned back north-northwest again. He traveled east on the badly pitted and pot-holed road until it turned into a dirt road, really just a trail that led into the jungle of the Rio Grande river basin.

Clay's destination was a small town on the Rio Grande river called El Gallo that had been mentioned several times in the notebook Clay had taken off the agency man's body.

One reference to El Gallo indicated a location about twelve kilometers north-northwest of it, labeled El Alberto Campo.

Finding a spot off the road John Henry backed the big sedan as far into the hole in the jungle as he could get it, some 60 feet in. Only the front grill showed from the dirt track of a road. He cut a few limbs and laid them upright then pulled vines and flowering limbs from around the car to mask the freshly cut limbs and car grill.

Satisfied with his handiwork Clay took a pistol and thirty rounds of ammo and the Uzi with three extra magazines. He left the shotgun in its hiding place in the trunk of the car, locked it and hid the key under the right front tire. He moved to the roadway, pulled out his compass and located himself on the Shell map. Then he shouldered the pack of rations and set out at not quite a lope toward El Gallo, a distance he estimated of about one hundred kilometers.

Clay followed the dirt track until full dark. Then he left the trail and swung a light weight nylon hammock between two trees, after cutting some little growth from between them. The jungle Clay was traveling through was not as thick as it would be later when he moved to lower elevations, but it was hot and humid with the cloying smell of jungle growth and blossoming vines.

Although he hadn't reached the Mosquito Coast yet, there were plenty of mosquitoes—the flying, biting types. Using some of his old reliable insect repellent he applied the goop liberally to his face, neck and arms, climbed into his hammock and without eating was fast asleep in five minutes.

The loud, raucous squawking of a large jungle bird woke him at daybreak, and as habit dictated, he lay perfectly still to better sense everything going on around him. Off in the distance he could hear the bellowing of a large animal, possibly a cow, and much nearer, the chattering of a band of monkeys. These noises along with the squawking of the large bird that had awakened him are reassuring as the presence of people would have silenced those noises.

He slid off the low slung hammock and did a quick circle of his camp. He saw only his own tracks in the soft dirt of the trail.

He rolled up his hammock and slipped it into his pack, extracting a can of potted meat at the same time. Making his breakfast of the meat and some awful crackers Whipple had thrown in he was soon past his passing out hunger phase.

Having finished his breakfast and taken care of nature's call he soon was on the dirt track headed for El Gallo.

John Henry had no plan of action other than to find the mysterious Striker, do him and get back to Bob Whipple's to pick up the safe deposit box key so he could get the information John Henry knew the chief had hidden away.

His confidence at what would happen when he found the Striker allowed no thought of anything other than complete vengeance, for Clay knew his capabilities in this line. He had long ago realized he was unique as a professional warrior, having undergone many baptisms of fire against other professionals.

Though he knew his capabilities were great he was also aware of several weaknesses. He was too stubborn for his own good and would sometimes pursue a lost cause too long. He also trusted his instincts and would make decisions too often based upon them rather than on the available facts.

Maybe combat had hardened him also to the point where he wanted to extract his own vengeance rather than leave it up to the "authorities." He really didn't know what his options were in this case, but instinctively he believed he should take care of it himself. An accusation against the man who had killed the chief would accomplish nothing. There were too many slick lawyers plus the great power of the CIA to hush things up. No, Clay thought, I'll find and do the Striker and then use whatever the chief hid to fight the agency.

Clay's movement along the small dirt track through the jungle was rapid but he was alert and as watchful as if he was on a combat patrol again. His eyes roved the terrain ahead and his ears were tuned to the normal sounds of the jungle.

He had been on the go for about four hours when he heard a loud roaring sound. He quickly turned off the little dirt trail and stopping under a huge Banyan tree, he sat his pack down and took out the nylon hammock. Then he crouched down and swung the hammock over himself and his pack, just as the heavy rainstorm hit. John Henry had been overtaken before by monsoon rains and had recognized the roaring noise as that of an approaching downpour that quickly transformed the trail to a swift moving stream of water.

He removed a can of food and opened it with his little P-38 can opener and while the storm and rain raged he calmly ate his food.

A half hour later the storm had calmed and settled down into a continuous steady rain. John Henry was soaked to the skin, from the rain and from his own sweat.

He took out a handkerchief and a small squeeze bottle of gun oil, compliments of Bob Whipple, and oiled his small pistol and the Uzi to protect them against the jungle moisture.

He put his pack back on and swung the hammock over his head and shoulders. Then he tied the handkerchief around the hammock and his neck, in effect making a crude nylon poncho with open sides where his arms swung free.

Clay swung out onto the trail, now a moving stream of water, and slogged ahead. After an hour of dealing with mud and in some places fast moving water, his resolve to keep moving toward his objective began to fade.

He was tired. His back hurt. And he was soaking wet despite the nylon hammock tied over his head and shoulders.

He had passed several trails branching off his trail, and now there wasn't much of a trail left for him to follow. The rain stopped and gradually the water running down the trial slowed and stopped, leaving a slippery mess of gooey mud.

Clay gave up fighting it and pushed through the wet, dripping jungle finally reaching a slightly higher and a little more open piece of ground.

There he pulled some branches down and tied the ends. Then using his nylon hammock to cover them, he made a small sleeping hut. He crawled inside, opened a can of beans, drank sparingly form his small canteen, stretched out on the pungent smelling carpet of dead vegetation and promptly went to sleep.

Loud voices in Spanish awoke him at daylight. He quickly crawled out of the hut, releasing his nylon hammock at the same time. He quickly rolled it up, stuffed it into his pack and checked his little pistol and the Uzi submachine gun. Then he swung his pack to his shoulders and eased out to the trail, but stayed off it. He saw nothing but the dripping wet jungle.

Glancing at the muddy trail he could see no one had passed by on it, so he eased through the heavy growth and vines paralleling the trail to his left. After moving about one hundred yards he heard a loud, impatient command in

Spanish, so he immediately sank to the ground and waited. Again he saw and heard nothing so he eased on until he became aware of the sound of a chopping axe.

He guessed that a group was advancing upon whoever was chopping. He continued his easy quiet movement, then suddenly heard excited voices and some shouting commands in Spanish. The chopping ceased with some desperate cries.

The frightened cries were in a language other than Spanish, followed by more Spanish, "Quien eres tu?" ("Who are you?")

John Henry eased his pack off, then crawled to where he could see the activity. When he got to the opening in the jungle it was as he had expected. A small military force, apparently Sandinistas for they were armed with AK-47s, were bullying two wood cutters who were obviously Indians. That they were frightened was plain to see and Clay could well understand why. The armed men in uniform were threatening, and even punching and kicking their prisoners.

Clay suddenly noted something that made him freeze. There were fourteen men in that force; that's too many for a squad and not enough for a platoon which meant there were more people around.

He glanced around and spotted a dozen or more Sandinistas advancing through the jungle. And he was within their area of advance.

He could stay where he was, which offered some pretty good concealment but not much cover, or he could try to move in front of them, staying ahead of their point men and hoping to find cover and concealment somewhere ahead. He elected to stay where he was hoping the woodcutters would provide enough distraction so he wouldn't be discovered. After all, his fight was not with the Sandinistas; more the opposite. He was stalking an agency man who was on the side of the Contras.

The United States contention that the Sandinistian government was communist was probably correct, for leftist and socialist regimes always seemed to show their true colors, or became communist after they come into power, like Fidel in Cuba for instance.

Clay remained absolutely motionless while the advancing troops did as he thought they might: they came together where the interrogation of the wood-choppers was taking place. One of the officers saw they had broken out of their combat formation and shouted some orders. The troops immediately formed a 360 degree perimeter leaving Clay outside their formation.

The interrogation had become brutal and it soon ended with the two Indio woodchoppers down on the ground apparently unconscious.

One of the interrogators pulled a small pistol and pointed it at the head of one of the downed men, but a sharp command from one who appeared to be in charge caused him to return the pistol to his belt; however, he delivered a sharp kick to the head of one, and another of the interrogators kicked and stomped the life from the other.

The group moved off to the north, settling into a rough, close diamond formation with the headquarters group close to the rear.

Clay waited until the sounds of their movement faded, then came out of his hiding place to check the wood choppers. He knew if he were smart he would back off and head east again, for some tactics of conventional forces operating against guerrillas call for leaving a squad to ambush anyone coming to see about the victims. Clay was incensed at the callous brutality displayed by the platoon of Sandinistas and he held his Uzi ready almost hoping some had stayed behind, but no one showed.

The men were dead. Their bodies were proof that the Sandinistas were bloodthirsty, for both were well past their prime and definitely non-military age, even to be members of the Contras. Their axes lay on the ground next to several logs of furniture wood similar to teak that were waiting to be dragged off or hauled, although there was no road nearby.

John Henry decided to leave them as they were for it was possible other woodchoppers would check on them and find their bodies. He stood up and looked around and saw what appeared to be a trail so he moved in that direction.

After moving south along the logging trail for an hour Clay came to a wide dirt road. From the signs this was where the logs were picked up and put on trucks to be hauled somewhere else.

The road ran east and west, and east was the direction Clay wanted to go, so he eased off the road into the jungle, found a downed tree and sat down on it and opened a can of ham and lima beans and ate it.

After what he had seen back there with the woodchoppers Clay was sure he didn't want to fall into the hands of the Sandinistas and from the packed down dirt road he could tell it was well used, at least by trucks, so it was likely to be patrolled by them.

Clay decided to follow the dirt road east but to stay off the road itself. This would allow him to make good time but not be caught out in the open unexpectedly.

He set out and spotted three passing trucks containing Sandinista troops in the next hour and a half. To Clay it was obvious they were trying to contain the Contras in the jungle and cut off their free movement.

Despite the stifling heat Clay made good time and by the next time he stopped to eat, in the early afternoon, he was well down in the Rio Grande jungle and, he estimated, within twenty kilometers of El Gallo. The road Clay was following was not on his Shell Oil map, but by extrapolating the distance he traveled and the directions he had moved in he believed his estimate was correct.

The jungle had become more dense, and the cloying smell of rotting vegetation blocked out the smell of the flowering vines and bushes. Although the day had been practically clear of rain clouds, Clay noted a gradual darkening and knew an afternoon monsoon rain was coming.

About twenty minutes later a distant boom of thunder caused Clay to pull off the edge of the roadway to seek shelter. He found an overturned tree with huge spread out roots. They made a nice, overhead shelter and Clay spread his hammock on the ground underneath them. He had no sooner finished getting positioned in his shelter when the rains hit.

He quickly stripped off his clothes and with a bar of soap in his hand stepped out in the rain. The falling rain was icy on Clay's bare body but invigorating at the same time.

He finished his shower, stepped back under his tree root shelter and scrubbed himself dry with a small towel. He dressed then ate a can of hamburger patties with rice, applied his insect repellent, stretched out on his nylon hammock and went to sleep.

While Clay was sleeping the rains ended and it got dark. When he awoke it was ten PM or 2200 hours military time. He was rested and refreshed and decided to continue along the roadway as long as it was heading toward El Gallo. There was almost a full moon and the dirt road made his march easy and he made good time. About one AM he could hear dogs barking, probably from the small town of El Gallo, and he could smell the river over to his right.

Clay left the road to the north and moved along a wash-out gully until he found a cleared area in the jungle. After bumping into several stumps he realized he was in a logged over area and went to one side and found two trees the right distance apart for his hammock. It took very little clearing between the trees and using his big knife like a machete, he quickly accomplished it.

He debated starting a fire to heat a can of rations but being so close to El Gallo he decided to eat his food cold.

About fifteen minutes later he covered his bare skin with insect repellent and crawled into his hammock. As he was drifting off to sleep he heard a coughing snarl, and quickly sat up in his hammock. The noise he had heard was a jaguar, the only one of the big cats that doesn't roar.

Clay remembered the tales he'd heard of the big cats. They are big, bigger than their cousin, the leopard, with much larger heads, jaws and a lot heavier in the shoulders.

The jaguar has a reputation of being a man-eater but Clay had heard how solitary animals actually follow along behind men "escorting" them from their territory. They eat about anything including domestic animals and stock, ground living mammals and even alligators. They love the water and are excellent fishers, slapping the fish out of the water onto the banks with their paws for later consumption.

Jaguars are solitary cats and only seek out other jaguars during the mating season. Soon afterward the male leaves and the female is left to bear and raise her young. At about six months of age the cubs begin hunting with their mother, then at about two years of age they leave her to find their own hunting territory.

Jaguars have brown spots, larger than the spots of a tiger, on a yellow coat, but solid black jaguars are not uncommon.

The male jaguars weigh up to two hundred fifty pounds and they hunt mostly at night on the ground, although they will climb trees and wait for their prey to come along.

The big cats are greatly feared by the natives of South America and they refer to them, almost universally as devils.

Clay thought, I don't need to meet up with any of these fellows, night or day. He waited, his pistol ready, and about ten minutes later he heard another coughing snarl, much farther away.

It reminded John Henry of the time he had been in heavy growth during ranger training and heard the rattle of a big rattlesnake, close at hand. He could not see his feet, so he froze and stood there absolutely still for ten minutes. Then he heard a faint rattle quite a way off, and it was as if the snake were saying, "It's OK now. I've left the area."

THIRTEEN

"If you are short of everything except an enemy, you are in combat."
Rule 16, Murphy's Laws of Combat

Even though Clay was sure the Jaguar had left the area the night before, he had been slow getting back to sleep. He was thinking of his self-imposed mission: the chief's killer had to die. To retaliate for their having the chief killed he would blow the whistle on the CIA as well.

The morning dawned with a heavy overcast and where Clay could see the sky it was filled with fast moving scudding clouds. The rains would come early today, Clay figured. He quickly ate a can of rations and moved out.

Bypassing El Gasso, he headed north using trails when they were going in the right direction and breaking through jungle growth when they weren't.

Clay was on one such trail when he heard a volley of shots. He took cover but after two or three minutes he moved again, coming upon a group of huts, four or five of which he could see. Seven armed men carried old U.S. carbines. One had a Thompson. They wore a motley collection of field uniforms including camouflage fatigues; all wore army green baseball hats.

Two bodies lay crumpled in a heap against the adobe wall of a hut. Three of the Contras, Clay supposed that's who they were, were dragging two natives, both military age males, to the wall.

The prisoners had their hands tied behind them. They were shoved roughly against the wall while the Contra in charge swaggered back about ten steps. Two others stood beside him. Then both aimed their weapons at their Indio prisoners.

At that point Clay was 12-15 yards from the firing squad. He had seen enough. He lay the Uzi down and aimed the .32. His first shot hit home in the nearest Contra's head. He made a slight adjustment and shot the second one in the forehead as he turned to look at his fallen companion.

For some reason the man in charge turned to face his men evidently not realizing where Clay's fire was coming from. John Henry shot him in the back of the head, put his pistol back in his belt and picked up the Uzi.

He moved toward the remaining four Contras guarding the Indians, while remaining concealed by the edge of the jungle.

Two men started for the jungle. When they were fifteen yards from him Clay stood up and placed well aimed fire in short two-three round bursts. Both men were down.

Clay looked for the other two and got a glimpse of them running into the jungle. He sprinted across the small opening and ran down the trail into the jungle. He saw movement ahead on the small path, and sprayed the area until his magazine was empty.

He continued forward with another magazine in the Uzi and almost stumbled on a body with three 7mm holes stitched up his back. There was no sign of the last man so Clay picked up the carbine the dead man had been carrying and retraced his steps to the villagers, some fifteen or eighteen including women and children.

Several women were crying over the two men the Contras had executed but the men were matter-of-factly going about the business of burying them.

One of the ones Clay had saved from the Contra firing squad spoke fairly decent English and it was as Clay had guessed, the Contras were using force and intimidation to recruit for their cause.

Clay told him one Contra had escaped but he wasn't too upset. The entire village was moving down river to the coast and would not come back here for at least six months.

He gave Clay the location of the Contra camp called El Alberto Campo along with two others, all some ten kilometers apart.

Clay asked him about the weapons but the Indio, whose name was Juyan, was emphatic; they did not want the Contras' weapons, for it would go bad on them to be found with them. Clay took everything: four carbines, a .38 caliber pistol and a Thompson .45 caliber sub-machine gun and all the ammo, and the man gave Clay some oil cloth to wrap them up into a bundle.

As Clay went out the north end of the village along the small trail, the villagers were streaming out to the southeast along another trail, leaving their huts empty and unattended.

John Henry followed the small trail where the one escapee had gone and found a rocky outcropping just a few yards off the trail. He took the oilcloth bundle of weapons and hid them in the rocks where rain would not fall on them. They would be hard to find unless someone knew they were there.

It was mid-afternoon and Clay took time out to eat a

can of food and the rest of those terrible Costa Rican crackers. Afterwards he stretched out on the leaf–covered ground with his head on his pack and went to sleep.

He was dreaming he was in Vietnam and the Cong had finally got him when a jab in the ribs with a rifle barrel woke him. There were several Contras, at least John Henry thought they were Contras, and all had their weapons pointed at him. One spoke to him in English, "Get up."

Clay got to his feet. They quickly searched and disarmed him, then searched his pack and even unrolled his nylon hammock. Finding nothing that interested them they marched him off up the trail he had been following.

About an hour later he was brought into a Contra camp, a distance Clay estimated was about seven kilometers from where they had captured him. That rankled him as he considered himself a professional and they had taken him without a fight and while he was asleep like a baby.

He observed his surroundings and he counted at least sixty or more rebels spread out in a village type camp. There were huts of all descriptions, mostly with tin roofs and sides made of woven grass fronds.

John Henry was already planning his escape and knew he would be able to push right through the sides of a hut. But he was not put in a hut. Instead he was put in a large metal cage with iron bars on the sides and top. Tin had been placed over the top to hold out the rain.

The camp smelled of human excrement and Clay knew their sanitary precautions were lax, to say the least. There appeared to be a community latrine, but from its appearance and smell Clay knew it was filled already.

Not too far away from the latrine was a cook shack. In addition to the raw sewage smell there was also the smell of burned beans. Despite having lived on cold canned goods for the past several days Clay didn't look forward to food from the cook shack.

The camp appeared to have no women and in looking around Clay saw no bunkers or fighting positions, indicating this group depended on flight rather than fight should the Sandinistas come.

John Henry was startled to see an American in a green beret, but then wondered at his surprise, for when he'd been in 'nam those three plus years, the agency had used the Special Forces as their military arm.

The leader of the group that had captured Clay came to the cage where he had been put, his hands still tied behind him, and asked questions about how he had gotten there. He even knew his name and did not appear overly angry about Clay's having almost wiped out one of his Contra squads.

He finally left after telling Clay that El Holliman, the "Striker," was being notified of his capture and would probably be there about daylight the next day. It was getting late in the day and Clay could see the Contras straggling to the cook shack for chow. He wasn't offered any food and would have refused it if he had been offered any.

Later an older Beret walked by and Clay called to him. The man came over. Clay introduced himself and the man said he'd heard of him. Then he asked Clay what was going on. Before Clay could respond the Contra leader charged back to the cage and in angry raw language ordered the Green Beret away, and to stay away.

Clay was surprised. Usually the Green Berets could do no wrong as far as the host country personnel were concerned. He was also surprised that the American accepted the severe rebuke and quickly left. The Contra leader glared at Clay then turned on his heel and walked away. Five minutes later a guard was posted a few steps from Clay's cage.

Just before full dark the older Green Beret and another one approached and began a discussion with the guard who self-importantly ordered them away. The two Americans scowled at the guard and argued some more before leaving seemingly without even looking at Clay.

There was an empty packing crate in the eight by eight cell apparently for the prisoners to sit on. Clay sat down and idly looked down at the floor. A K-bar knife lay in front of him. Clay was positive the knife had not been there before so he knew it had been pitched in while the Berets were talking to the guard.

Clay moved his left foot and the knife was out of sight. He considered the situation. The door to the cage had an old style padlock on it and John Henry knew instinctively the guard would not have the key. The floor was solid wood planks and the bars were about 3/8" re-bars, set in holes drilled through the wood floor. If that was all that was holding them below, it's possible he could whittle the bars loose with the K-bar.

Clay knew that if the bottoms were loose and not welded to metal he could bend the re-bars out enough to get through. In fact, if there had not been a re-bar welded to the middle of each bar all the way around, he could have pulled them apart enough to slip through.

The mosquitoes were fierce and Clay asked the guard to give him his inspect repellent from his pack, which had been tossed down just outside his reach from the door of the cage. The guard happily told him to "shut up."

It was now so dark Clay could barely make out the guard even though he was just four or five steps away. He crouched on the floor next to the empty packing crate and found the knife, fortunately getting it in his hand hilt first.

He held the knife in his fingers and turned it inward guessing, as his hands were tied behind him, that the sharp edge was against the half-inch nylon rope.

He had trouble getting any motion into the knife but just about the time his fingers were getting numb from sawing the sharp edge of the knife across the ropes, he felt a twinge as the blade went through the rope and nicked his other wrist. The ropes fell away and Clay gingerly pulled his hands from behind him. Not until feeling returned did he realize how tight his bonds had been.

His wrist was pouring blood, so he lay the knife on the packing crate and wrapped the wrist tight with a strip of material from his shirt. Then he stretched out on the floor and lightly shook the re-bar bars. They were indeed loose. He took the K-bar knife, and stuck it into the hole one of the bars was set in, and applied pressure. There was a squeak and the board split leaving the bar hanging loose.

That was the only easy one. Clay spent the next three hours getting four more bars loose from the heavy timbered floor. He finally applied his heavy shoulder muscles to the bars and pushed them out enough to slip through. Then, taking the time to crawl around the cage for his pack with the map and compass and his insect repellent, he crawled on all fours toward the opening of the trail he had been brought in on.

The weather was overcast and little light from the almost three-quarter moon broke through. Clay had no problem finding the opening but almost immediately he lost the trail in the inky blackness. He spent a lot of time on his hands and knees trying to find the hard packed foot path that he was constantly losing in the darkness.

Several times Clay heard what sounded like large animals in the jungle on either side of the path. He knew huge anaconda snakes in the mosquito coast attacked even large animals. A large twenty footer had attacked and killed an eight foot caiman. One was caught recently that was an unbelievable 77 feet long!

He was particularly fearful of getting off the trail onto the east side where there were huge marsh areas with three- and four-feet-long eels that could shoot up to 700 volts of electricity through the skin of their bellies. They lay in the marshes by the thousands, and only the Indians were brave enough and knowledgeable enough to go in there after them. These eels had been known to crawl onto an eight foot crocodile and shock him to death.

Clay got off the trail but guessed right and found it right away. He listened to the night sounds that were worse than traffic noises in a big city. Monkeys in the double canopy above squawked, screeched and chattered and off in the distance he heard a cough-snarl from a hungry jaguar.

While he listened Clay fumbled around in his pack for his bottle of insect repellent and liberally applied it to all the parts of his body he could reach. Finished with that he pulled a can of food out, opened it and gulped it down. He was famished but didn't want to take any more time from his flight from the Contra camp. He wanted to get to the weapons he had cached just before they had captured him.

He stepped off up the trail again and had not taken more than ten steps when he heard clearly, too clearly, the commotion in the Contra camp. They had just discovered he was gone.

Clay moved on and for about fifteen minutes the trail ran straight and he made good time. But it couldn't last, and did not. He soon found himself thrashing around in vines, heavy ground cover and thorny bushes of all kinds.

He realized he was not making any progress trying to follow the trail and he had gotten off the path again on the west side. The ground seemed to be rising so he made an effort to continue going "up" into the jungle. After about twenty minutes of climbing, mostly on his hands and knees, he reached some large out-cropping of bare rocks, and climbing behind one he found a level spot. He stretched out with his head on his pack and blocked out the jungle noises and went to sleep.

At dawn John Henry woke to the very familiar whump-whump-whump of a helicopter flying low over the thick jungle. He could not get a look at it but he knew it was a Huey, a HU-IE, and he wondered if it was armed. If it was and they used it to try to locate and eliminate him, he was in trouble, big time. It could be though, that it was just a chopper bringing in the Striker. If so, Clay needed to get a weapon, for his mission was to eliminate him in spite of his rebel group of Contras and the Green Berets with them.

While the dawn was changing into full light Clay ate another can of food, then made a quick reconnoiter of his location. He was in heavy jungle but on a small knoll or hill quite a bit above the terrain where the trail and the Contra camp, El Alberto Camp, was located.

Although being up above did not give him any better visibility, it did make it easier to pick up the sounds from down below. He could hear troop movement but he doubted he could get to the trail before their lead elements got there, so without a weapon he would have to move in front of them and not worry about the trail down below.

He took out his Shell Oil Company map but it was of no help as it showed nothing but jungle. He tried to recall every turn in the trail from when they had captured him but could not remember any major change in directions.

The trail they had followed was some ten degrees east of magnetic north; therefore he would have to go on an azimuth of 190 degrees to get back to where he had hidden the weapons.

From the sounds at the camp he believed he had made about two kilometers last night so if his previous estimate of going about seven "klicks" or kilometers, was correct he needed to move five kilometers along 190 degrees, then take a jag of about two hundred yards to the east. Clay wasted no time. Picking up his pack and holding his compass out in front of him, he began his trek through the heavy jungle.

Clay made good time for a little over one klick because he was on a higher elevation, but his axis of movement led him back into the lower elevations and its heavier jungle growth. The sweet cloying smell of rotting vegetation got worse as he moved down, and the squawking of the jungle birds and monkeys made it difficult to hear the Contras who were undoubtedly scouring the jungle for him.

He soon became very thirsty as the Contras had not only taken his weapons and his knife but also his canteen. But his thirst had to wait for even a few swallows of water from any of the stagnant pools he ran across would bring him down in a matter of hours, unless he could boil or treat it for drinking.

Coming up to a small opening in the jungle Clay sensed some danger and looked at the open area. It was about ten feet across but ran for about a hundred yards then curved south out of his view. The surface was covered with green grass and looked like a mown lawn. Clay picked up a heavy broken limb about three feet long and pitched it unto the grassy surface. In a few seconds the stick was sucked down and out of sight. The "grass" was just the surface of a deep pool of water.

Clay turned east and followed the pool. When it went south he continued to follow it until it ended. Clay picked up a dead limb about eight feet long and pushed it into the "pool," to see how deep it was. The limb was immediately snatched from his hand and sucked down through the "grassy" vegetation on top of the water.

Nicaragua has many active volcanoes. As a consequence there are blow-holes in the surface of the land. This one had tapped into an underground stream and had a vicious undertow. But the vegetation intrigued Clay.

Clay remembered a grass in Vietnam that noise or vibration would flatten out but that would rise up again in a few minutes. If a man was brave enough to stand up quickly after a sniper on the ground fired, he would see a row of grass lying down all the way to the end of the sniper's rifle.

Clay had been so intrigued with this grass that when he came back to the States in 1966 to go to the Infantry Advanced Course he gathered up a twenty by ten inch wide hunk of the sod and put it in his small carry-on bag. When he went through customs in Tan Son Nhut before boarding the commercial aircraft, the customs agent asked what it was. Clay could not resist his sudden impulse to pull the man's leg a little, and told him it was his pet grass that he had trained to do tricks.

Of course the customs man was thinking Clay had been over there too long, so Clay said, "Look, I'll show you." With that he clapped his hand over the grass and said loudly, "Lay down." The grass immediately flattened out. The customs agent's eyes got big and he yelled to another American to come over and look. The other American customs agent came over with a Vietnamese interpreter.

The grass had stood up again so Clay did it again and the grass flattened out. The second American said, "Well,

94

I'll be damned," but the Vietnamese fellow just poo-pooed and said, "Very many grass like that in Vietnam," and he pointed out the window to a grass line along the fence. "Same, same," he said. "Vibrations make grass lay down."

Both custom agents were ticked off and the one said, "No way, lieutenant. You can't take any kind of 'grass' back home." At that time grass was an euphemism for marijuana. So Clay had to leave his "pet grass" behind in Saigon.

But now he got busy setting a trap for the Contras who were searching for him. He went back to a spot just before the curve in the pool. Then, using his K-bar knife, he cut a rough "trail" through the jungle back toward the trail. He was a little surprised to find he was only some 60 yards from it so he cut right up to the edge of it, then he ran back to the pool, followed it around the curve and back up the other side and lined up with the fresh cut path he could see on the other side. Then he started cutting again. To someone standing on the other side of the deadly open area it would appear that Clay had crossed the open area and continued cutting a path there.

He cut in about ten feet and then stepped over to the side to eat a can of meat. He had just finished when he heard a group of Contras coming, evidently following Clay's fresh cut "trail."

John Henry could not believe how big a success his ruse was. The first three men coming at a dead run hit into the grass covered water and were immediately sucked down and out of sight. Two others stopped in time and just stood there in shocked confusion at what had happened to the first three men of their group.

Their loud clamoring in Spanish soon brought someone with some rank who walked to the edge of the pool as he listened to the two excited men. Using the barrel of his rifle he pushed onto the grass. It opened for a second. He saw the fast moving waters and quickly stepped back. He said something in Spanish and all three turned and headed back toward the trail.

Clay had a small measure of satisfaction but the facts were still the same. He had no weapon, no water and not much food. Worst of all, the Contras were searching the whole area looking for Mrs. Clay's boy, John Henry. He picked up his pack and headed south.

FOURTEEN

"Men acquire a particular quality by constantly acting in a particular way"
Aristotle

The jungle was thick but John Henry was able to move fairly well thanks in part to his jungle training, and also to the many animal trails and woodcutters' paths he had run across following the 190 degree azimuth. So far he had spotted four of the huge anacondas; one he knew for certain was over thirty feet long, and that reinforced his desire to stay the hell away from those buggers.

It had been over two hours since Clay had heard anything of his pursuers. He decided he was far enough ahead of them to go to the trail, so he turned left and in less than three hundred yards he found the trail and headed down it at a distance-eating pace.

About forty-five minutes later Clay found where he'd left the trail just before he had been caught. He checked the area thoroughly and saw no sign the Contras had come back to lay in wait for him. After he had circled the entire area he went to where he had hidden the weapons. They were gone!

There was absolutely no sign of anyone having been there in the two days, but the oilcloth wrapped bundle of carbines and the Thompson submachine gun had disappeared. Clay knew there was no mistake as to where he had hidden them, and he was positive the group that had captured him had not found the weapons.

Clay wasted no more time there but went back to the trail, turned south and headed for the Indio village. He arrived fifteen minutes later. The huts were still empty.

Although the Indians had told him they wanted nothing to do with weapons, for fear of the Contras and the Sandinistas, Clay searched the village looking for some kind of weapon. He did not want to make the four day trip to the CIA sedan he had hidden just this side of Sebaco.

He found no weapons in the village, nor did he find anything that would be of help to him, except a small well. Clay tasted the water. It was delicious but still he drank sparingly.

He also found some beans growing up a trellis on the back of one of the huts. He picked off enough to fill his previously almost empty pack, eating them raw as he picked.

After picking his beans he looked around some more and found a wrecked, and destroyed old vehicle of some kind. It was nothing but scrap metal but Clay picked around and came up with four feet of good electrical wire. He also pried apart the old rear springs and took a leaf spring with small screw holes on each end.

The spring was three feet long and had a curve of about three inches on each end from straight line. He pulled off a board from one of the huts, then moved to a vantage point where he could watch the trail and most of the village.

He then started to build a crossbow, using the four-inch board as the main frame. Using the K-bar knife, he cut a notch on the top of the board three inches from one end, that was deep enough to take the spring. He measured and found the center of the spring and pressed it snugly into the notch with the ends curving back to the rear. He cut a groove along the top of the board that was three feet long and one half inch deep.

He used his knife to whittle a pistol grip within three inches of the rear end of his crossbow frame. Then he cut an inch and a half wide notch behind it that was wide at the top but narrow at the bottom.

Finally he made a triggering device. When the bottom was pushed by the user's thumb the top of it would rotate backwards lifting the bow string off the back of the notch, and firing the bolt.

His board had several small nails sticking in it when he had pulled it off the hut, and one of these driven through the trigger made the pin for the trigger to rotate on when raising the string.

After John Henry finished his bow he made four three foot long shafts, with bird feathers in the ends to stabilize them in flight to the target. Now he would fire-harden the points to eliminate the need for an arrowhead.

Clay went back into the village and, picking out the smallest hut, one that had fire wood next to an indoor fire pit, he closed the makeshift door and settled in. He hung his nylon hammock almost by feel over the one open window.

Within minutes Clay had a fire going and his crossbow bolts placed where the points would get maximum heat without the arrows catching fire. He found several old pots and quickly snapped some beans and hulled others, to put into one of them. He filled the pot with water, put the last can of food, hamburger patties, into it and put it over the fire using a hook there for that purpose.

While his beans were cooking Clay turned and rotated the arrows and soon was satisfied that he now had all the elements for a good working crossbow.

The old electric wire made an excellent bow string and fastened through the small screw holes and drawn up tight, the bow was almost too strong to be drawn comfortably, but Clay was not looking for comfort. He tried the cross-bow, without an arrow in the notch, and when the trigger released the string he heard the twang he wanted. Clay knew he now had a killing weapon.

An hour later Clay swung the pot off the fire and as soon as it had cooled he ate almost all his bean-hamburger mix. It was delicious. He saved just enough for morning then put out his fire and took the hammock from the window.

The three-quarter moon lit the bare area of the abandoned village so well that Clay could see the opening of the trail some one hundred yards. He hoped the smell of the cooking beans had not reached too far away but he knew just how far smells could travel.

He had lain on ambush for hours at a time and then suddenly been alerted by the smell of fish and rice, or by the strong foul-smelling cigarettes the Viet Cong and North Vietnamese preferred.

He had planned to sleep in the jungle but thinking it through he thought he would probably be better off in the hut where he was and hopefully he would pick up on any sounds or a change in the on-going sounds, if the Contras came. Besides, he would not like having several coils of anaconda snake around his body.

Clay found hooks in the wall for swinging hammocks. He put his up, put on some inspect repellent and went to sleep. He was awakened a few hours later by a sudden silence and he moved to the window.

The moon still beamed down but now there were long shadows from the huts and the trees in the village. As Clay watched he saw a figure cross a moonlit spot and enter the deep shadows of the next hut over from his. He continued to watch and caught a glimpse of a figure entering the shadow of the hut he was in. He quickly drew the string on his crossbow, put an arrow on it and waited.

There came a scratching on the closed door and a voice. "Senor, it is I, Juyan."

Clay recognized the voice. It was the Indio Clay had saved from the Contra firing squad, the one who spoke good English.

Clay moved to the door, holding his crossbow at the ready. He eased the door open and Juyan quickly entered. A moment later he pulled a .38 caliber pistol from under his shirt and handed it to John Henry. It appeared to be the one he had taken from the Contra running the firing squad. Clay now knew the Indio had followed him and removed the weapons he had hid.

The Indian quickly made his allegiance known by telling Clay there were at least six Contras at the edge of the jungle near the trail opening and three more on the other end of the deserted village right inside the jungle's edge.

Juyan told him they knew he was somewhere in the village from the smell of his beans, but he did not know why they were waiting to search the little village.

Clay thought he knew. He would be very surprised if a large force wasn't being organized to make sure he did not get away again. He figured he had until dawn before they got there.

John Henry told Juyan what he was thinking and asked about another way out.

Juyan told him there was a way going east, but a deadly way and one that only he, Juyan, could take him through. Also, it would have to be after daylight.

Clay and Juyan took John Henry's gear, including the old pot with his remaining beans, and slipped out of the hut and through the shadows as Juyan had done when he came to Clay's hut.

They entered the jungle on a small path on the southeast end of the small village. The path must have led to the little community's toilet area, for Clay could smell the old excrement. Just inside the edge of the jungle they stopped and hunkered down in the dense foliage to await daylight some two hours away.

Clay loosened the string on his crossbow but kept it and his four arrows close at hand. Neither Juyan nor Clay had anything to say and in a few minutes Clay had drifted off to sleep sitting with his back to a large tree. He was instantly wide awake though at the familiar sound of a Huey helicopter.

Clay glanced through the bushes at the village. Every hut could be seen, although the moon had gone down. It was breaking dawn and the chopper was obviously headed their way, just as he had surmised it would.

A few minutes later a smoke grenade rolled out from the edge of the jungle into the largest opening on the south end of the village. A moment later a camouflaged painted HU-1E helicopter flared out and sat down, its rotating blades blowing the green smoke away, and Clay could smell the familiar smoke as it was blown past him there at the edge of the jungle.

Troops poured out from the still settling chopper, ten in all. They took up a 360 degree perimeter as a husky, white man dressed in faded khahi with a gun belt strapped on and carrying what appeared to be a Uzi with a folding shoulder stock, came out. He had corn-yellow hair and was big, as big and broad as John Henry.

He shouted a command and the seven Contras Juyan had told Clay about appeared out of the jungle edge, along

102

with three more at the end closest to Clay, near the trail entrance to the village.

Clay fumed for he knew that if he had a weapon, other than the pistol Juyan had given him and his crossbow, he could have picked off the Striker and finished that part of his mission. But he had no weapon!

The helicopter rose and headed northwest toward El Alberto Campo probably to get more troops. El Holliman was going to saturate the area with Contras and run him down.

Juyan was whispering to Clay that it was time to go, but Clay hated to leave the man who had killed the chief. "One minute, amigo, I want to see what happens next."

The troops, operating in two-man teams began to check the huts. Clay could see the Striker moving further away instead of closer.

Juyan tapped him on the shoulder suddenly, and pointed. One Contra had espied the small path and was approaching. Clay pulled the bow-string back, notched an arrow, and waited.

The man, ahead of his partner, hesitated at the opening of the path but took several steps in and apparently spotted scuff-marks in the soft soil of the path. He started to turn. Clay's hand-made crossbow twanged and the arrow hit the man in the upper chest with a loud thump. He fell backwards, his eyes wide and staring. There was no other sound.

Clay moved to the body and removed the man's magazine vest with its twelve magazine pockets, and put it on. Then he picked up the U.S. Army carbine. It was an M-2, which had a selector switch that allowed the user to fire full automatic.

Juyan grabbed the feet and Clay the shoulders and they carried the body about ten yards into the jungle, off the path.

Returning to his former spot at the edge of the jungle Clay looked for Holliman, but only got a quick glimpse of him at the other end of the village. The troops had fanned out and were checking the edge of the jungle for fresh signs and Clay saw three headed his way.

The chopper returned and came in to land. The first two troops out had dogs and Clay knew it was time to move out. He motioned to Juyan, who looked greatly relieved. They moved quickly down the path past the village toilet with Juyan leading the way.

The Indian soon slowed and then stopped. He turned to Clay and whispered, "Place your feet exactly where I place mine. One misstep and you will be eaten."

Clay looked ahead. The path had disappeared, except for scattered bare rocks. In between was the strange grassy vegetation he had seen earlier. Juyan picked up a stick and poked into it creating instant turmoil. There appeared to be millions of snapping, slashing, scraggled–teeth fish. Clay wondered if they were the deadly piranha he had heard so much about.

Juyan went forward, carefully placing his feet on certain spots that only he could see. Clay could not see any difference in the terrain but he had seen Juyan's demonstration and he was very careful to place his feet in the exact same spot.

They finally came out one hundred yards further along and Juyan said, "Is okay now. We have a distance of five hundred steps there" he pointed generally north, "and about one hundred steps there," he pointed south, and about fifty steps there," and he was pointing to the east.

Juyan added, maybe we stay here one day or two day 'till bad men gone.

"Will they come here, amigo?"

"No, senor Clay. Maybe one or two will try but they will die and the others will turn back."

Clay and Juyan sat watching the way they had come, although they could not see where they had entered the deadly path. Clay pulled his pot around and offered Juyan some of the beans, but the Indio shook his head and Clay thought he would probably turn up his nose at even fresh cooked beans with the greasy hamburger patty mixed in.

Clay wasted no time but dug in and finished them off and enjoyed them immensely. He stood up to stretch when he heard both the dogs baying on their trail. There was a single "yip" then an anguished scream from a human throat then silence.

Juyan and Clay looked at one another. No words were necessary. The two dogs and at least one man had fallen prey to the vicious piranha fish, if that was what they were.

Clay picked up the carbine and released the magazine. It held twenty rounds but one was in the chamber and Clay pulled the operating handle back and ejected the round. He looked through the barrel and found it to be relatively clean. He inserted the extracted round into the magazine and pushed it into the receiver until it locked into place. He then put the safety on and worked the operating handle again. A round was picked up from the magazine and slid into the chamber. The selector switch was on full automatic and he left it there.

Clay sat back down again but he thought he knew what would happen next, for had he been in Holliman's shoes that would be what he would do. He would crank up the "Huey" and put some gunners in the door and fly tree-top level, criss-crossing the area and shooting everything that moved, especially believing his prey was unarmed.

John Henry was not wrong. Soon he heard the whumping of the chopper coming their way. Clay instructed Juyan to hug the base of a big tree and not to move. He himself moved away from the big tree to the edge of a small clearing no more than six or eight feet across. He flipped the safety off the carbine and waited.

The chopper came across the watery death trap that was clearly visible from the air. It made a turn over the jungle island and it hovered seventy-five or eighty feet up, a door gunner with a 7.62 mm machine gun mounted on a rod projecting up from the floor of the bird, began "hosing" the area.

The rounds were cutting limbs and ricocheting around, and he heard a loud moan from Juyan, but he held ready as the chopper rotated in the air, all the while continuing its hover, so the other door gunner could do some firing.

When the chopper made its turn it was above Clay. For a long moment he and the second door gunner looked at one another. Then Clay's carbine spat out a full magazine of twenty rounds in a continuous roar of sound.

The gunner folded over, only a belt strap held him in. The burst however had splintered the plexiglass and the aircraft commander, or number one pilot slumped and the chopper turned almost up on its side.

Clay saw Holliman sitting in the back row of seats at about the center as the chopper commenced righting itself, and he swung the carbine toward him as the last round fired. Clay changed magazines, stepped farther out into the little clearing and centered the floundering chopper in the sights of the .30 caliber carbine. Although he was out of sight of Holliman, he held the trigger back. The carbine roared again and the limping chopper belched smoke going away as Clay's second magazine went empty.

Clay swore softly and muttered, "That bastard's living a charmed life." He went over to check on Juyan and found him hunkered down behind the trunk of the big tree. He was unharmed but frightened silly and Clay could see why as there were twelve or fifteen holes in the tree and bushes had been cut down by the bullets hitting all around him.

Clay got him by the arm and pulled him up saying, "You're okay amigo, you're okay."

Juyan finally stopped trembling and in answer to Clay's question said there was another way off the jungle island. "One other way, senor Clay, but many crocs and we will have to go now for any later and we will be caught by the lover." Clay asked him to repeat "lover" and he said, "rain storm, senor, rain."

Clay looked up through the vines and tree tops. It was indeed becoming cloudy and overcast. He picked up his pack and his crossbow but left the now empty pot behind.

With Juyan leading the way they headed north. Soon Juyan stopped and gave his "step where I step" warning, adding "We must go very fast as crocs have young this time of year and they are very aggressive."

Then Juyan turned, stepped out on a rotting log, ran half the length of it and jumped to a rock some three feet away. As soon as he landed Juyan looked all around for crocodiles.

Clay concentrated on putting his feet where Juyan had put his as they moved along a lagoon that did not have any vegetation covering it. As they moved, Clay spotted a dozen or more of the huge reptiles, all of whom appeared to be paying a lot of attention to them.

When they came to the top of a large berm, three crocs slid off it and into the water. Clay noticed that although Juyan appeared to be calm he was constantly watching the huge beasts.

Juyan said, "Very dangerous, senor Clay," and he pointed back at the "path" they had just run across where several of the bigger crocs were climbing up on the solid earth. "The children of the village run this path, sometimes jumping over sleeping crocs, as a game." Then after a pause, "Sometimes croc is no sleep and we lose child."

Clay could understand the young boys wanting to risk danger to prove their bravery but he felt he would play hell jumping over one of those monsters.

After they moved north for several hundred yards, Juyan stopped and said he must leave and rejoin his people. Then he asked Clay if he needed the other weapons. Seeing his embarrassment at having stolen the hidden bundle of Contra weapons, Clay told him, "No, amigo. I have one weapon and it is enough."

The Indian pointed north-northwest and said, "El Alberto Campo maybe three or four kilometers that way."

Clay thanked him and said, "Juyan, I'm John Henry Clay. I'll be here until I can kill El Holliman. If the Contras bother you, come find me and I'll help you fight."

"Gracious, senor Clay. We hope to stay away from them and the Sandinistas. Both are very bad!"

The fun and games were over. Clay was after the Striker and the Contras would be wise to stay out of his way.

FIFTEEN

If it's stupid but works - it isn't stupid.''
Rule 3, Murphy's law of Combat

Clay cleaned his carbine on his first break from walking through dense jungle. Then he inserted a fresh magazine and moved the selector switch to single shot. That meant he would have to squeeze the trigger every round he fired. He had never been big on full automatic fire except when he needed to put out a lot of fire quickly, as on the Striker's chopper.

Clay had been plowing through thick jungle for over an hour generally going on 347 degrees. He knew he was on the east side of the trail from the Indios village and El Alberto's camp. It was hard to estimate distances traveled but he felt he was within one kilometer of the camp. Clay was relying on the camp's lax security, even though they had come up with dogs that morning, so he was planning to be alert.

The already darkened sky opened up and Clay slipped under a large Banyan tree, pushing up under its dangling roots. He pulled his hammock over his head but still had a lot of cold rain hitting him. It was really pounding down hard now and all he could hear was the heavy rainfall.

About an hour later it seemed to be letting up and Clay could see farther out in the jungle. He left the nylon hammock over his head and gathered his pack and weapon and set out again. He wanted to approach the camp during the rain; as it was he broke out of the jungle right beside one of the Contra huts.

He could see people in the big cook shack and knew they could see him so he tucked his hammock around himself and boldly walked past the cook house, not even looking that way, and got out of their sight near the big cage.

Clay was surprised to see it occupied. Stepping up closer he saw the two Green Berets who had helped him escape. His position was not all that much better than theirs but he was incensed that they would be thrown in there, and decided he would do something about it.

He stepped up closer to the cage, actually out of the rain as the over-hanging tin roof extended about three feet from the bars. As far as Clay could see there was no guard. Both men had their backs to him and were hunkered together, sitting on the same packing crate.

"Hey, Sneaky Petes, What's happening?"

Both men turned and the older Sergeant said, "Shit, it's that John Henry Clay character. Man, how come you're not on a boat going back to the States?"

Clay laughed and said, "I heard the Contras can't catch anyone else to put in their cage so they decided to pick on someone easy, like a couple Green Weenies too dumb to resist."

"You're partly right, man. That CIA guy, Holliman, was some upset that you got away and the last ones near the cage was us, so, we're here waiting for him to decide what he wants to do to us. He's even talked of a firing squad! I don't put it past him. He's crazy!"

110

"How about your team captain? What Holliman's doing is illegal and your officers should be getting you out of here."

"They're young Weenies, John Henry, and they're scared to death of that guy and the agency."

"Okay, guys, do you want to stay in here or do you want me to get you out?"

"How'll you do that?"

"I just might go get the main guy at this place and order him to turn you loose. Or I might put this carbine barrel in the lock and see if I can spring it."

"Whatever, John Henry, but you'd better hurry 'cause the rains letting up."

Clay looked around. Sure enough he could see much more clearly, so he moved to the padlock and inserted the barrel of the carbine. One small jerk and the lock sprang open. He removed it and checked the barrel of the carbine; there was no damage.

He said, "Let's go. We need to have a talk with your team officers." The three briskly walked through the camp, John Henry with his carbine ready and the selector switch on full automatic.

They came out the north end of the complex where there were two small "hooches" with sand bags up to the bottom of the windows and all the way around. From what Clay could see in the rain, the area was clean and combat ready. A fighting position, not quite a bunker, was between the two huts where six or eight men could hold the place against a much greater force.

The two sergeants led Clay into the first hut where they found a very young captain and an even younger first lieutenant. There were also three more "older" sergeants and another younger one.

The captain was a maverick officer named James Oberdorf. His lieutenant was Henry "Hank" Harris.

Clay wasted no time. He gave his name and launched right into his story. He finished by saying that he was bringing some justice to the agency's killers first and foremost, but that their own mission there was in jeopardy by their allowing the CIA to drive a wedge between the Americans and the forces they were supposed to be organizing, training and advising.

The captain, though young, was a fine specimen of Special Forces manhood. He was square-jawed and had black, curly hair and big arms and shoulders. His sharp, green eyes were intelligent and his quick response to Clay's story was emphatic.

"By God! I knew I should have done something about it but that damned CIA man said he'd have my ass if I messed up our "working" relationship with the Contras."

"That CIA man is dog meat when I catch him" Clay said. "Your problem, however, is to reestablish the proper relationship between your Contra force and the team."

The young captain said, "I've heard of you John Henry, and I welcome your advice, but unfortunately your CIA guy limped out of here today on that sick chopper. They replaced some oil hoses to let them fly the thing but their Aircraft Commander is badly wounded and the door gunner / crew chief is dead. They headed for Honduras just before the rains."

"Damn," John Henry said, "I did want to wind up this mission."

"I wasn't in on all of it but I don't think Holliman's coming back anytime soon. He said he'd "work from the other end." He told the Contras to keep after you, and promised them a big American money reward."

"Here's what I think we should do. We arm everyone and walk in on El Alberto and any of his troops around, put them under guard and tell Alberto we're going to execute him for not cooperating with us Americans. Then we let you decide to give him another chance. That should reestablish your authority in helping them against the Sandinistas."

"I'd like to clean up and get some clean clothes. Maybe a set of "jungles" from one of you that's my size?"

"No problem, sir. We'll have your old rank sewed on by the time you get out of the shower," the older sergeant said.

After a shower, shave, fresh underwear, a clean set of jungle fatigues and a pair of new jungle boots, Clay felt whole again. The team had M-16s. Clay asked to borrow one and was told it was his. It came with six filled magazines of ammo.

He and the team of ten men locked and loaded, got into a loose squad diamond formation and moved into the main camp. The rain had ended but the dripping water and sounds of the nearby jungle still covered the sound of their boots on the muddy camp paths.

The day was getting late and Senior Sergeant Ross, the team sergeant, said Alberto and his staff would be in the mess hall, so that's where they headed.

They arrived at the cook shack and mess hall and with no ado marched in and aimed their rifles at all the Contras in the place, some thirty or forty men. John Henry, the captain and the older sergeant who had been jailed walked to the head table. John Henry's rifle went to the man's chest.

Clay said, "Senor Alberto, you have been found guilty of high treason for imprisoning members of the U.S. Army Special Forces sent here to help their allies, the Contras, against the oppressive government of Daniel Ortego and his Sandinistas."

Clay looked at the man's face and eyes and knew his ploy was working. He went on, "The penalty for this offensive action is death by firing squad. We will execute you now. Who is to replace you?"

El Alberto tried to get up but Clay's M-16 pushed into his chest and he sat back down, "But senor, I have done nothing but follow El Holliman's instruction," the panic–stricken Alberto said.

Clay said, "You mean you took instructions from a renegade CIA man over your own allies?" Clay sorrowfully shook his head, wondering as he did if he was laying it on too thick.

The man was pleading now. "Senor, I did not know he is a renegade. Of course, Captain Oberdorf and his team are our allies and I meant nothing to interfere with our mutual goal of eliminating the Ortego lackeys from our country."

Clay began shaking his head as if to say it was too late, but Captain Oberdorf broke in with, "Sir, is it absolutely necessary we execute Senor Alberto? Up until now he has been a brave fighter and leader against the enemy." And he looked at Clay questioningly.

Clay said, "Captain, I've seen these people before who believe the U.S. Army is secondary to the CIA. When the agency killer comes back he will take up with him again. No! I believe swift justice is called for here."

He was interrupted by El Alberto, now pleading his case, "No senor, we will obey the CIA only on the instructions of our Special Forces Advisors. Please senor, let us start out anew."

Clay looked at Captain Oberdorf and said, "Captain, I leave it to you but I would advise that if the renegade

CIA man, the Striker, returns to this area he be detained or executed for his crimes." With that Clay turned on his heel and marched from the mess hall while the group of Contras started open mouthed.

Back at the hooches about twenty minutes later Clay was being congratulated by Captain Oberdorf and Lieutenant Harris. But despite his success Clay was far from jubilant; he was still back at square one in his efforts to run the Striker down.

The Intell Sergeant briefed him on the situation in Nicaragua. He knew elections were to be held soon but he had been told that former President Jimmy Carter and a contingent of United Nations personnel were in the country to observe the elections; also two– and three–man teams were going all over the country to the polling places, unannounced. So far, Ortega apparently was abiding by the agreement to hold free elections.

Clay did some thinking and decided that when Holliman said he would "work from the other end" he might have meant that he was going after Karen and Bob Whipple back in Costa Rica.

He told the team he would head out the next morning for the agency auto he had hidden near Sebaco. They decided to send a squad of seven men with two senior sergeants along with him.

By daylight the next morning they were on their way, heading southwest on a more direct trail, to Sebaco. Six hours later Clay realized the squad was moving as if they were in a friendly area.

He pointed this out to the older sergeant, who looked a little embarrassed, and said, "We've tried everything but they just won't put out security, or even a scout."

"I saw the Sandinistas operate," Clay said "and they do put out security and flank guards. If we run into that unit I saw we'll take a black eye."

115

Clay barely finished speaking when the Contras were taken under fire from the front and east side; Clay saw two Contras go down under the initial volley.

Clay had hit the ground at the first burst of fire. He gave a short whistle and motioned to the older sergeant that he was going to the left to try to flank the Sandinistas, who, except for the heavy jungle, had them pinned down.

Clay quickly crawled on all fours in a great half-circle finally advancing to the sounds of rifle fire. He had been given back the .32 caliber pistol and when he came up behind the pair of Sandinistas who were putting flanking fire on the Contras, he pulled it from under his shirt, pushed the safety off with his thumb and shot both of them in the back of their heads.

He crawled past them and soon had about eight Sandinistas spotted. They were well spread out and Clay knew he wouldn't be able to get them with his pistol so put it away.

He put the selector switch of the M-16 on full automatic and sighted in on the closest enemy, took a deep breath and squeezed the trigger.

Clay rode the muzzle of the M-16 up, holding it on full automatic and raking the enemy down as they rose up in panic. He put four down then quickly changed magazines and caught seven or eight more rushing south away from his devastating fire. More than half went down. He kept placing fire down the trail although the enemy was completely out of sight.

The last round fired and Clay looked around at the bodies, some piled together and none moving. He carefully reloaded and moved to another vantage point but saw nothing.

"Sergeant," he called out. "I think they've left. But leap frog the men forward while I cover the area."

116

"Yes, sir." Then to the Contras, "Okay, move up like you've been taught." In a few minutes Clay saw four contras advancing two at a time, staying spread out and not getting too far in front of their partners in a good firing position.

It's remarkable, Clay thought, how a little combat brings home the training. Clay yelled at them to take up a perimeter when the Contras got to the last pile of bodies. He stood up and saw a slight movement from the corner of his eyes. He immediately dropped to his knee and "hosed" the large bush on his left.

A Sandinista dropped his weapon and fell forward. Clay swung his M-16, ready to spray anything that moved. Nothing happened, however, as the faint wisps of gun smoke hung in the air and stung his eyes.

The quiet of the jungle was very unnatural; Clay could even hear his own breathing. The rancid smell of rotting vegetation co-mingling with the smell of fresh burned cordite from the fired ammunition almost carried Clay back to jungle engagements in Vietnam, and fresh pain hit him as he knew he would never again hear the chief's confident, gravely voice on the radio, as he flew in "soup" above the jungle. He had been one helluva airplane jock and a fantastic friend.

Clay and the Americans took a quick count. There were fourteen enemy dead and blood stains on the trail leading away. The Contras had suffered two killed and one slightly wounded.

The Americans told Clay it was another twelve or fourteen hours moving through criss-crossing trails through the jungle to Sebaco. Clay told the sergeants to take their squad and their dead along with the captured enemy weapons and return to El Alberto's camp. He told them he would go alone and thanked them for the escort this far.

"Okay, sir, we'll get going. If the Striker comes back we'll throw his ass in the cage and hold him for you." The Sgt. Major grinned as he said, "We'll put a different lock on it too." They shook hands and Clay set out bearing southwest hoping to find the trail where he had left the car.

SIXTEEN

"A great part of courage is the courage of having done
the thing before."
Ralph Waldo Emerson

That night Clay camped right off a trail leading exactly where he wanted to go. He slung his hammock, ate some MREs (Meals, Ready to Eat) the Berets had given him, covered himself with insect repellent and got into his hammock.

The jungle night sounds were loud but they could not drown out the steady roar of the mosquitoes. He was reminded of an old friend who had been stationed in the delta in 'nam. He said one night he was on a patrol and was slapping mosquitoes, and one stood up and slapped him back. Another friend had chimed in he knew the mosquitoes were big 'cause the day he arrived he had seen one with a saddle slipped off to its side and he knew it had thrown its rider.

Then others told how they had seen delta mosquitoes "mating with turkey buzzards." It was gallows humor because the mosquitoes were as fierce in 'Nam, as they were here.

Clay was on the trail by daylight, every sense alert as he moved toward Sebaco. That Sandinista unit had lost a lot of men on an ambush they themselves had set, and chances were they had hightailed it back to their camp. On the other hand they could be waiting along any of the trails Clay was following, just thirsting for revenge.

That wasn't the case however, and Clay hit the trail he was looking for not more than a "half-klick" from the agency car and it was only about 1600 hours or four pm in the afternoon.

He carefully reconned the area making a full circle around the car before approaching it. Everything was as Clay had left it and he removed the camouflage, recovered the key and drove off toward Sebaco.

The towns Clay drove through retracing the route he had taken in coming from Costa Rica were full of people. The voting was in full swing.

The Sandinistas controlling the traffic were trying to maintain a hands off neutral position so they waved him through check points without asking any questions.

He even gassed up at the same service station and was pleased at the more congenial "Gracious, senor," and a big smile as he tipped the fellow an American dollar.

Suddenly Clay had a sense of forboding. He had been feeling good, even though he had not yet wrapped up the Striker, but now, the hair on the back of his neck was tingling.

He had had these hunches before and he reacted by pushing the gas pedal to the floor. The big sedan responded and he went through the open border full bore, the wind screaming in his ears from the small wing windows.

He left the Pan-American highway with a tire-squalling, sliding turn and as he neared Bob Whipple's driveway, his intensity was almost overwhelming.

John Henry might have missed the small opening except for a loud explosion that he recognized as a hand grenade. He swung into the short roadway and cut the ignition just in sight of the house. The big sedan continued to barrel up the drive.

He braked and opened the door just as a gunman swung toward him and let loose a long burst from a small sub-machine gun. His shots shattered the windshield. John Henry dived out of the car, rolled once and pointed the M-16 toward where the man stood. When his bulk filled up the front sight he stroked the trigger and sent a three or four round burst into him.

Not waiting to see him drop Clay swung toward two other men who were hunkered down facing the house. Both turned, bringing their weapons up, and Clay's M-16 commenced cracking, sending a stream of 5.56mm bullets over them both. They were swept down and Clay could see another body lying at the edge of the porch.

The whumping of a helicopter sitting idle on the east lawn drew his attention and he spotted two men running toward it. One was Holliman. He stood up and directed heavy fire from the M-16 toward them, but after a short two round burst the bolt clicked on an empty chamber.

He quickly inserted a full magazine, jacked a round in and aimed toward the chopper again, but it was too late. The two men had leaped madly through the open doors and the chopper swung to the east and low-leveled away.

Clay dashed to the front porch, flattened out next to the blown out door way. He yelled, "Bob, Bob Whipple! It's Clay! Are you all right?"

Karen yelled back, "Clay, there's a lot of them, be careful. Bob is hurt but I think he'll be okay."

"There's four dead and two left on the chopper, but I'm going around the house. Just sit tight."

John Henry circled the house, going from cover to cover right from the book. He got back to the front and yelled again.

"Karen. It's John Henry. I'm coming in."

She yelled back. "Hurry!"

Clay hurried in and found she had wheeled Bob to the big sofa and somehow had got him onto it.

Whipple was pale and drawn looking and there were bandages high up on his right shoulder. He also had a bandage, slowly turning red, around his head. He was unconscious.

The young gardner, Juan, stuck his head in the door and rattled something in Spanish. Karen said, "Bob's regular doctor is at the hospital in San Jose. He's getting the number for us and will bring Bob's station wagon to the front since he's not sure that sedan of yours will move. It's pretty shot up."

Two hours later Bob was in the hospital. The initial examination revealed they had gotten him there just in time. The prognosis for him was good and Karen said she was going to stay with him.

John Henry sensed Karen was in love with Bob. He examined his feelings about that and concluded that despite his deep friendship with the chief he was pleased. Karen deserved happiness.

His quest for vengeance for the chief's death appeared to be stalled. The chopper Holliman and his men used for their attack and for their getaway had low leveled east then swung west, gained altitude and headed south off the coast and over water. This indicated it was based in Panama. He decided he would head there. If the agency's sedan made the trip he would return it.

SEVENTEEN

*"Justice is the constant and perpetual wish to render
every man his due."*
Emperor Justinian

John Henry trusted his instincts, and the long years of army life with constant exposure to danger had given him a kind of ESP, (Estra Sensory Perception). That ESP was telling him the Striker was on the defensive and that now was the time to crowd him.

Although the man was a deadly killer, Clay was sure after all his failures he was running scared. He had deserted the field of battle twice in his efforts against Clay and that indicated cowardice. Clay had an opportunity to observe a case of pure cowardice in Vietnam.

A Military Intelligence (MI) unit of ten men was attached to Clay's B Team of Special Forces. The senior master sergeant in charge of the unit was interrogating several prisoners the Berets had brought in. Clay, who had just returned to the base camp and left the chopper, heard terrible screaming.

He hurried to the prison compound and found the senior sergeant "talking long distance" to a prisoner.

"Talking long distance" is what they call a form of torture where electrodes are put on the prisoner's testicles.

Then the other wire is hooked up to a EE8 hand crank telephone which puts out a charge when cranked.

Clay was furious. He wanted the information the man had, but he did not torture prisoners and no one else in his command did.

He had the senior sergeant stripped and wired him up telling him that he was going to make an example of him. The sergeant broke down, blubbered and cried, and begged Clay not to do it.

Clay had no intention of doing it and was sickened at the behavior for the sergeant. Only later did he learn the prisoner had been tortured out of his mind.

Clay sent the entire team packing. A few hours later he received a call from an irate Lieutenant Colonel Helmes, the MI detachment commander.

The colonel demanded to know by what authority he had sent the team back and he threatened to have Clay courtmartialed.

Clay said, "Colonel, they were violating the Geneva convention concerning treatment of prisoners of war. If you wish to pursue it, however, I will prefer charges against your entire unit. We have one male prisoner who has been tortured completely out of his mind. And we have no proof that he was Viet Cong."

The colonel quickly backed away and told Clay he respected his judgment in the matter and guaranteed nothing like that would happen again. No further attachment of MI personnel took place while Clay was the B Team commander.

Clay, having seen cowardice, sensed the Striker was losing his killer's edge. It was time to crowd him and the agency's detachment in Panama.

Clay told Karen he would send Juan back with the station wagon. He was going back to Panama. He told her to tell Bob he was taking the safe-deposit box key and letter of authorization with him. With that he collected the gardner and they drove back to Whipple's house.

They buried the four bodies in Bob Whipple's little cemetery. Then Clay checked the big agency sedan. It had lots of bullet holes but no real damage.

The tires were okay and Clay could see to drive so he collected his things, told Juan to stay in touch with Karen at the hospital and headed for Panama.

Clay arrived in Panama and went through the gate at Howard Air Force Base with just a wave-on by the Air Policeman. The agency sedan had the right bumper stickers he guessed.

He drove to the Base Operations building on the flight line and after parking looked around. There were two C-130s and since Clay had not noted the tail number of the aircraft he had flown in earlier he had no way of knowing if one of these was the agency "bird."

He went inside to check the operations lounge waiting room hoping to spot some of the agency people he had met with the chief on his ride to La Paz from Santiago.

He saw no one he recognized and turned to leave when a tall, familiar looking airman came from the restroom. Clay took a second look and recognized Saul, the crew chief on the C-130 Clay had flown on.

Saul saw him at the same time Clay recognized him. Shaking his head slightly he walked past him and out the door. Clay looked around then turned and followed him out.

Saul stopped between two large oleander bushes, looking about him as he spoke.

"Sir, we got reamed out big time for allowing you to ride back with us. First, the CIA came around then the Wing Operations Officer, Colonel McClure, bashed us good for allowing a civilian on board our military aircraft. But shit on him, anyway."

"Damn, Saul. I'm sorry. I guess technically I am a civilian, but after sixteen plus years as a dog-face I tend to forget that I'm now a silly-villain.

"Have you made any progress finding the chief's killer?"

"Yeah, I know who did it and who ordered it, but I'm having a time pinning the son of a bitch to the wall. That's the reason I'm here. I'm looking for the agency chopper that was used yesterday against Bob Whipple, another friend of the chief.

"It went 'feet wet' in this direction with the striker on board. Do you know where the agency keeps their aircraft?"

"They have support from here at Howard and do their refueling here, but their two choppers are kept on their pads behind the embassy in Panama City."

Clay got directions to the Embassy from Saul, shook hands with him and left.

Clay stopped on the way and picked up a bag of what he called Mexican food: tacos, tamales and other goodies. He then drove to the chief's house and really wasn't surprised to find only a pile of ashes and rubble. The agency had made sure nothing was hidden in the house.

A neighbor was watering his flowers and Clay walked over to him. Nodding at the rubble he asked, "What happened?"

"Two Norte Americanos, set fire and vamoosed. One big, senor, as you are, with *amarillo* hair. A *lubio*, you know, blond hair. The other was small man, like a *rata*, you understand?"

Clay nodded and the man said, "I tell police all this. They not do anything to catch *ratas*, you understand?"

Clay said, "Senor, I think I know the *grande rata* and I will see to him personally. Senor Thompson was *amigo bueno.*"

Clay needed a base of operations and thought of Karen's house but he had no key. He remembered Karen's tall, good-looking school teacher friend and decided to find her and see if he could use Karen's place.

He drove to the school but all he could remember were her first two names, Mary Beth. When he told the woman at the Administration Office who he was looking for she said, "Sure, you mean Mary Beth Coleman. Her class is over in five minutes. I'll let her know you're waiting to see her."

In five minutes a bell rang and a minute later Mary Beth came running up to him. Her trim form and quiet beauty reminded Clay he had not shaved or bathed in three days, really bathed that is, in five days.

He explained he was looking for a place to hole up for a few days and thought of Karen's place. Mary Beth said Karen had called her and told her Bob was doing fine. She giggled as she said that Karen was sure he would be by to see her.

Clay got that sinking feeling people get when they're being manipulated. Mary Beth was a beautiful woman, and maybe after Clay's mission was completed he would come back to see her, but now her attention made him a little edgy.

She rummaged through her purse and came up with a key. She used a piece of scratch paper to write the address down for him, but he knew he would not need it. If he had ever been to a place once he could always go back to it, even in the jungle.

"Maybe I should come by this evening to make sure you've found everything?"

He didn't know why he answered that would be nice. Probably to allow her to see him looking a little more presentable.

Clay drove to Karen's house and entered. He felt the chief's presence there as if he were waiting for John Henry to report he had "off'd" his killer.

He sat down on the end of the couch and for about a half hour simply stared at the blank wall in front of him. Grief and sorrow filled him for his friend, killed for trying to give him a helping hand, an old buddy who was down on his luck.

Clay had lost a lot of good friends in combat. He had always reacted vigorously in retaliation against their common enemies but had not grieved as he now grieved over the chief. He swore he would make that killer pay.

After a short while Clay went through the house and, turning things on, soon had hot water for his bath and shave.

He opened the closet door in the spare bedroom and there were the chief's clothes.

The chief had been an inch or two shorter and several inches bigger in the waist, but Clay found some bleached-out jeans that were not a bad fit, plus sport shirts, gabarra shirts and some pull-overs that would cover the .32 caliber pistol.

None of the chief's shoes fit but Clay found shoe polish and brushes and before bathing he cleaned and polished the almost new pair of jungle boots the Berets had given him.

After a hot bath, shave and a strong Johnny Walker scotch and water, Clay felt good again. After the one drink Clay put the bottle away. He had climbed out of the bottle and he was not going back into it.

After a short nap Clay was up and dressed and when Mary Beth knocked on the door at 1800 hours, he was ready to go out for dinner.

Mary Beth was dressed in the frilly shirt and peasant blouse preferred by women in South America. Her face was bright and shinning, and she wore a perfume that did things to John Henry's libido.

Clay put the safe-deposit box key in an envelope, sealed it and took a stamp from Karen's desk. He addressed it to himself at his post office box in Bal Cove, Florida. They dropped it into a mail slot near the school.

Mary Beth was indeed a beautiful woman and John Henry found himself wanting to impress her as he gave her step-by-step description of his chase after the chief's killer.

When he mentioned Karen's feelings about Bob Whipple she immediately agreed. During Karen's telephone calls to Mary Beth she had gone from deep sorrow for the chief, to her last call when she used the term "we" in speaking of her and Bob.

She ended by saying, "I hope Karen doesn't get hurt again. I know she loved the chief but she needs someone to be around all the time, someone she can do for."

John Henry described Bob Whipple—a robust, healthy man and soldier now living out his days in a wheel chair. It led her to say, "Maybe that's who Karen needs in her life. She certainly didn't need a roving, drinking soldier of fortune like the chief."

Clay got the idea that Mary Beth had been glad Karen had a love in her life, even though she disapproved of the chief's job and life style.

Mary Beth talked, he learned she had run away from a broken love affair, and, speaking fluent Spanish, had taken a teaching job with the Canal Zone Company. She was in her second year of a three–year contract.

John Henry did not know why he found this information so important. He did know Mary Beth aroused deep yearnings in him.

After their dinner Clay decided to use Mary Beth as a sounding board, so he put forth his objective of getting the Striker separated from the agency and eliminating him, hopefully with great pain.

She went ashen. "You mean kill him?" she was horrified.

"Mary Beth, this man has killed and killed and he's under the protection of the CIA, one of the most powerful agencies in the world. There is no way to make him pay legally so I must kill him for his crimes." He went on, "After that I take the information the chief has hidden away and go public with it to get back at the agency."

She exhaled. "But to kill a man. There must be another way."

Clay's analysis of Mary Beth was undergoing drastic changes. There are people who cannot adapt to, or even to conceive of, the cruelties of the real world. He had hoped she was not one of them.

He himself had never been able to understand how people could die or undergo serious injury to themselves rather than hurt another human being. He was reminded of Karen's fierce desire for revenge, until she killed one of those who killed for a living. At that point Karen's desire for revenge ended.

Clay shook his head as if to clear the cobwebs, and they dropped the subject then, and went on to talk about Clay.

Clay surprised himself by saying, "I think I want to get into law enforcement." As he said the words Clay knew it was true. When this was over he would pursue a career in police work.

They finished their after dinner coffee, settled the tab and went to Mary Beth's car. She drove them to Karen's and pulled in behind the agency sedan sitting under Karen's carport.

It was dark and the fragrance of the flowering vines filled the air. Clay suddenly realized the porch light that he had left on, was out. He reached to the small of his back under the pull over shirt for his pistol when several flashlights came on. Four hand guns covered them.

A heavy voice said, "If he makes a move kill them both." Clay had never heard the Striker's voice but he immediately knew who was speaking. Instead of Clay catching him it was the other way around. The Striker had caught Clay.

Clay reluctantly removed his hand from under his shirt and quick hands did a body search for weapons. Even Mary Beth was not spared the patting down.

Holliman and his group put them in two of the now familiar sedans and drove off in the one Clay had been driving.

They were taken through winding, back streets to a small bungalow set back off the street and with no homes close by.

Inside the house they were handcuffed—Clay's hands behind him and Mary Beth's in front—and shoved into what probably had been a bedroom. Now, the room was empty. A heavy metal grating covered both windows.

Clay stood quietly in a corner waiting to see what would happen next. After a few moments the Striker came in with five men.

Holliman gave orders and three men left to return at eight AM in the morning. The other two were evidently to be their guards.

The Striker faced Clay and said with a smirk, "You gave me a chase man, but I got you." The two other men laughed. John Henry stood quietly wondering why he had not been killed already.

There was a heavy rap on the door and one of the men left the room. He returned leading a gray–haired, medium–built man, and two companions, obviously CIA agents.

He walked over to Clay. "So this is the son of a bitch who's been giving us so much trouble. Hell! He doesn't look like shit to me." He went on, "Has he talked yet, Carl?"

The Striker, whose name Clay had put together as Carl Holliman, said, "No, sir. We haven't had time to interrogate him yet."

The man glared at Holliman and said, "Get to it. I want everything he knows about what the chief had, and before morning." He stepped up to Clay and with no warning punched him. Despite John Henry's quick head turn to ride with it, it brought shooting stars to his brain. The man smiled a thin lipped grimace and said, "You son of a bitch," we'll teach you to screw around with us."

He left saying, "Call me when you have everything. Then kill them."

Holliman escorted him to the door mumbling, "Yes, sir. Will do, Sir."

The door shut and the Striker was back. He stood in front of Clay, and said, "Make it easy on yourself and the young lady, man." He hit Clay again but not as hard as the older man.

Clay could have taken him out right then with a karate kick to the groin, but there were the other two and one had his .32 out.

Clay knew any one could be broken, but he knew he could last as long or longer than anyone. He was silent, but promised himself that if he could last long enough he would have his day.

Mary Beth had been quietly crying the entire time and now she came in for some of the Striker's cruelty as he casually back-handed her, and drove her to her knees. "Shut up, bitch."

One of the others stepped up to Clay and delivered a heavy blow to his midsection. When he didn't go down the Striker swung a haymaker that cracked like a rifle shot to Clay's jaw. Only his "riding" with the punch so fast it wasn't noticeable saved him from a broken jaw.

For three hours he was slapped, punched, kicked and hammered by one of the guards and the Striker.

Holliman was covered in sweat and some of Clay's blood was smeared on him when he called a halt to the beating.

"Let's work on the bitch." Then both of them started slapping her down then dragging her to her feet, then slapping her down again.

The Striker said, "Maybe the bastard will talk if we take turns with his woman."

He grabbed the terrified and bruised Mary Beth and dragged her out of the room. Clay could hear her anguished cries, and finally a scream, then silence except for the rhythmic pounding of a sweaty body making a meaty sound as the Striker raped the unfortunate Mary Beth.

The sounds ended and the Striker returned dragging the almost nude girl behind him. He looked at Clay and said, "You stupid bastard, are you gonna talk?" There was even more sweat on him now and drool oozed from his mouth.

Clay was silent knowing he could do nothing and any threatening words would be worse than useless. His eyes fell upon Mary Beth. She was looking at him and she said, so softly he could barely hear her, "Kill the bastards, John Henry."

Although her voice was just a whisper the Striker heard her. He swung a wicked blow to her head and she went tumbling head over heels unconscious.

The Striker waved to the guard who had been helping him beat Clay, and said, "Go ahead. Get a little from the bitch."

The man pulled at his belt until Holliman said, "Damn it, not in here. Take her out on the couch." The man then picked up the young woman and hurried from the room.

The meaty pounding started up again and although Clay was mentally prepared he had to grit his teeth as he stood quietly and waited.

At no time during the last three or four hours had the other guard put his pistol away. Whether he had been instructed to have his pistol out and ready, or whether he sensed Clay was a lot more dangerous than the others thought, Clay did not know.

The second man returned to the room dragging the almost unconscious young woman, and Holliman said, "I'm gonna go get cleaned up some and get us some coffee. Keep at him but don't let the bastard die on us," and he left.

The man who had kept his pistol out the entire time looked at Mary Beth's almost completely nude body and licked his lips. "My turn," he said. The man put his pistol in his back pocket and dragged Mary Beth from the room.

The first man stepped up to Clay and punched him in the stomach. Clay leaned forward with a grunt, although the blow scarcely hurt him, and when he started back up again his head and upper body went back and the toe of his right foot, encased in the steel toed jungle boot, came straight out and up, catching the man under his chin.

Clay had practiced that kick for over fifteen years and did not have to look to know the man was dead. In fact, a check of the man's spinal column would reveal it was completely broken, and the head was being held to the body only by the skin and muscle of the neck.

Clay squatted. By hunching his body down, each time pushing his arms down further under his rump, he finally got the cuffed arms to the lower side of his thighs.

He sat back down on the floor and brought his arms and hands over his feet and legs and up, and just like that his cuffed hands were in front of him.

Clay would hear the meaty pounding as the second man, as he was mentally calling them, continued raping poor Mary Beth.

Clay got to his feet and hurried to the body and pulled the .32 pistol from the man's side pocket.

He checked to make sure a round was chambered, released the small thumb safety and stepped to the door.

John Henry peeped through the opening where the door wasn't completely closed. The man was lying on Mary Beth with his back to him and his head facing away. He grunted as he hunched on Mary Beth's supine body.

Clay pushed the door wide and stepped through, put the pistol to the man's head. His eyes widened as he realized what was happening.

Clay stroked the trigger and the man's body jerked sideways while his head burst like an over-ripe water melon.

Mary Beth opened her eyes and gave a short scream. Then she started trying to get from under the dead man's body.

Clay pulled the body off her averting his eyes as he did so. "I'm sorry, Mary Beth, but there was nothing I could do earlier."

She said, almost in exasperation, "John Henry I know that. I'm sorry I was such a big baby."

He looked at her. One eye was black and almost swollen shut. She had marks and bruises all over her face and body, and now she was trying to make the few strips of clothing still on her, cover everything. He gave her an admiring glance. "Mary Beth, you've got guts." He added, "let's see what we can find for you to put on."

Clay searched both bodies for the handcuff keys. Neither man had them, but the first man had a wad of several thousand dollars, and he surmised this man was a cartel man probably on loan to the agency.

The other bedroom had a few items of men's clothing, probably Holliman's since they were all extra large. There also was a large wooden frame bed with a foot board of thick wood. He placed his hands on either side and drew the hand cuff connecting chain tight. Mary Beth took one of the pistols from an inch away and pulled the trigger. The chain was blown in two. One of the sections flew back over his hand leaving a bad bruise across the top of it.

Mary Beth put on one of Holliman's long tailed shirts and used a tie to tie it up tight around her waist like a belt. She looked good in the get-up and Clay told her so. She said to him, "Shouldn't we be trying to get away, John Henry?"

Clay knew he shouldn't be putting her in more danger, but he wanted the Striker and he would be returning soon.

He said, "Mary Beth, I want to kill Holliman, not only for what he did to the chief, but for what he did to us tonight.

"This is my best chance and I've got to wait for him." He went on, "Could you catch a taxi and get out of here?"

136

She looked at him in her solemn way and said, "I wouldn't be of any help if I stayed, would I?"

"No. I'd be concerned about your safety. It's better if you get out of here."

"All right, John Henry. Will you call me?"

"Yes. You see, I have plans for us."

She blushed, as much as she could with all the bruises and said, "Kill him, John Henry. But make him know he's dying first."

"I will." He leaned down and lightly kissed her bruised lips.

Clay said, "There's no phone here, Mary Beth, how are you going to get a taxi?"

She said, "I know where I am and there's a taxi stand just about a block away." She reached up, touched him on the cheek lightly, and turned and headed for the door.

"Wait a minute." Clay cautiously eased the door open and looked out. There was nothing in sight, and no sedans either. She went through the door and in a few minutes disappeared in the darkness.

Some fifteen minutes after Mary Beth had left, Clay had both the dead men's pistols, silencers affixed, and was waiting in the darkness of the shrubbery in front of the house. Although lights were on in the house it was dark where he hid. A large sedan that Clay was very familiar with pulled up into the driveway.

As Clay stepped forward he saw, not the Striker, but the CIA man who had slapped him so hard earlier.

He still had his bodyguards so Clay stepped back into the bushes, at the same time a stab of flame accompanied by the now familiar cough of the silenced .32s came at him from the hedges to his left.

John Henry knew that the ever alert Striker had returned and found something amiss and had set up his own trap, with only chance bringing the CIA Chief back at that time.

Clay looked toward the car. The CIA Chief was on the ground on the far side of the car, his door hanging open. His guards were on the left side.

Clay was in a mess so he decided to try to even the odds. He promptly shot both guards, one after the other, just as the Striker screamed out, "It's the prisoner! He got loose and he's armed! He's up in the bushes to the right of the door!"

The Striker blazed three more shots, in a searching pattern with the little pistol making noises like some one grunting.

Clay felt a sharp, burning pain in his left thigh and sent a shot at the Striker's flash.

He fell to the ground and from there could see the CIA man crouching on the other side of his car. Clay lined up the sights and triggered off two rounds and saw the man collapse to the ground.

Clay knew the man was hard hit or dead and turned his attention again to Holiman in the hedges to his left. He held a pistol in each hand. When one was out of ammo he would fire with the other.

EIGHTEEN

*"Chance is perhaps the pseudonym of God when he
did not want to sign."*
Anatole France (Le Jardin d'Epicure)

Suddenly he heard a rustling in the hedges closest to
him. He swung that way but did not fire. Nothing more
was heard and Clay figured the Striker had thrown a stick
or rock to draw fire from him.

Clay lay perfectly still willing to give his foe the first
move. His patience paid off. A dark shadow separated from
the hedges and sprinted toward the back end of the big
sedan parked in the driveway.

He triggered two shots at the fleeing shadow which
sounded like one cough. Then he rolled two rolls back to
his left where he had been standing when he was hit.

There was no return fire. He felt strange being in a
shootout without the sound and fury of weapons being
fired. Now he watched both sides of the sedan hoping to
see the Striker if he moved away from it.

He was totally surprised, then, when the car started
up, the front door slamming hard and loud, and screeched
backwards into the street. The rear door was still hanging
open as Clay spent his last three bullets in a futile effort to
stop the Striker from escaping.

Alone on the "battlefield" Clay examined his thigh wound. Luckily it was only a burn that had almost quit bleeding. He checked the three bodies; only the CIA man who had slapped Clay so hard, was still alive. He was hard hit in the stomach and through his right shoulder.

Clay rolled him over as gently as he could, and removed his pistol. It did not have a silencer on it but he found one in the jacket side pocket for it.

Inside the man's billfold was the little identification folder they all carried. He was Charles Longstreet Special Agent, CIA.

The man's eyes flickered, "Longstreet, why'd you have the chief killed?"

The man moaned, then whispered, "He talked too much."

"Who gave the termination orders? Did you order it or did Miami order it?"

The man said, "Big Hand told me to use my ... my own judgment. I ordered him killed." He moaned again, "God, it hurts so much. Are you going to call for an ambulance?"

Clay answered him with just a little sorrow in his voice, "No, I'll stay with you until you die, but I'll not call an ambulance. You see, you killed a friend of mine and you have to die for that."

He groaned and said almost in a whisper, "There's a contract out on you so you'll die also."

"Longstreet, your contract killer, the Striker, just isn't up to the job. Three times we've shot at each other and three times he ran. He just scooted out of here in your car. You see, he was in the hedges and knew he couldn't leave on foot across the lawn for I'd see him, so he came to your car, sneaked in and tooled off, leaving you behind."

"The bastard," Longstreet breathed, then coughed and died. Clay dragged the bodies inside and stripped them of money, guns and I.D.s. He also found a set of car keys in the pocket of the second man he had killed while he was raping Mary Beth. Clay knew the Striker had left his car parked somewhere nearby and had left in Longstreet's. These might be the ignition keys.

Clay glanced at the watch he had recovered from one of the agents. It was 0330 hours. He remembered the Striker telling his other three men to be back at 0800 hours so he had five hours if he wanted to ambush them. Clay had nothing against them and, since the chances of the Striker coming back were slim, he decided to leave.

Taking the weapons and everything he had taken off their bodies, he turned the lights off and stepped outside.

Clay stood there for a long time, savoring the smell and fragrance of the oleander blossoms and the sweet smell of morning air unpolluted by the carbon monoxide of car exhausts.

He eased through the darkness to the street and followed it west. About one hundred yards down he came upon the Striker's car and considered. Was it a trap? If so Clay could not see how it would work.

He peered inside. Nothing. He dropped down and looked for explosives under the front of the car. Then he looked under the back.

He found nothing so he opened the door carefully then reached inside and tried the keys. They did not work. He kept the weapons, a fairly large pack of them, and the money, dumped everything else on the front seat and walked away.

Mary Beth had said there was a taxi stand nearby, but he did not find one. After over an hour of walking, though, he was again in the downtown section where he soon found a restaurant.

The few patrons and the cook and waitress stared at his beat up appearance but he ignored them and had a good breakfast of three eggs, bacon, toast and coffee so strong he almost had to chew it which was exactly the way he liked it.

It was now just a few minutes past five AM and he was tired so he looked for a taxi.

He had the man drop him off at Karen's house, but when he tried to enter he found he had no key. The Striker had removed everything from his pocket and when he had picked up all his stuff at the CIA safehouse he had recovered his money, wallet, small pocket knife and wrist watch, but not Karen's key.

He moved around the house and found an unlocked window. He cautiously went through the entire house and found nothing had been touched.

The light was beginning to shine in and he made sure every window and all the doors were locked. Then he stacked pots and pans in front of each entrance door, giving him an early warning device if visitors came. Then he lay down on the bed, placed his weapons on the pillow beside him and went to sleep.

Clay dreamed wild dreams of fire fights that he could not seem to get a handle on and of long dead friends, all telling him, "John Henry, watch out for the jaguar."

The chief's voice, although Clay's dream didn't bring up his face, was there telling him, "John Henry, I need to be avenged. You've got to get my killer for me."

Most of his dreams were about finding the chief's killer but Clay also dreamed about his young son who, even during the early years of his life, had been taught that nothing John Henry had ever done was right.

In this dream John Henry could see a young teenager, who looked like him, telling his friends, "My old man? Hell! He's one of the all time losers." Clay wanted to grab him and shake some sense into him. Tell him that what he was doing, what he had done in combat, was good. It was done for his country.

A burning sensation woke him up. It was muggy hot and perspiration had gotten into the scratch wound on his thigh.

It was 1600 hours. He had slept for almost ten hours. He heard a car door slam and immediately grabbed the Uzi.

He was standing, ready to spray the front door when it was pushed open, scattering pots and pans with a loud clatter. Mary Beth pushed her head in and looked around.

She saw Clay in just his shorts, the Uzi held out in front of him, ready to fire. He pulled the weapon up but something in her posture alerted him, plus the fact that her bruises and cuts had not been treated.

He stepped forward as she raised her voice and almost shouted "Clay, are you here?"

He grabbed her arm, yanked downward, and the Uzi chattered over her head at the man standing right behind her. He continued to hold the trigger back as he pushed the weapon forward and let it spray behind the one he had just killed.

There was the sound of ricocheting bullets as some hit the agency sedan parked in the drive. Clay saw a second man fold up as several rounds caught him in the stomach and chest.

The explosive noise from the rapid-fire sub-machine gun was almost deafening. The last round went out of the barrel and Clay dove head first out the door, over the body of the first man who was lying half in and half out the door.

He shifted one of the pistols to his right hand as he hit and rolled. He saw a brief movement from the corner of his eye and swung the pistol to it. The three coughs it made were almost a symphony as all three bullets caught a big man coming at a run. The man dropped his own pistol and walked several steps with his hands clutching where the bullets had caught him in the stomach and chest.

As the man fell dead in front of Clay he heard the sound of running feet, Clay dashed out past the end of the agency car, leveling his pistol as he ran but he got only a quick glimpse of dirty blond hair as the Striker went out of his sight.

He swung around with the pistol out in front of him, but all three men were dead. He heard questioning voices and doors slammed as people came out of their houses to investigate the noise from Clay's Uzi. Clay leaped to the last man he had killed and pulled his body out of sight.

Nothing could be seen from the street nor the other houses. People looked around but even before Clay started back inside Karen's house, they were headed back inside also.

Mary Beth lay on the floor, motionless. His breathing became constricted and he mouthed *oh no,* as he rushed to her.

Clay checked for bullet holes or other new injuries. There were none. He checked her pulse. It was strong, if a little rapid, and he guessed she had fainted.

He picked her up and carried her into the bedroom. Her eyes blinked and she regained consciousness as he lowered her to the bed.

"John Henry, are you all right?" She said trying to sit up.

"I'm fine and so are you so just relax a minute."

She lay back. "They made me come here, John Henry. God! You must think I'm a rat to betray you, like that. I didn't want to." The last was almost a wail from her bruised mouth.

"Hush, Mary Beth. You gave me the warning I needed, and except for the Striker they're all dead."

She said, He got me when I left you this morning. He thinks you're his own personal devil. He thinks he has to kill you to escape." She added, "He was raving and said the four of them were the last of Operation Big Hand, whatever that is." She waved at the bodies at the front door and said, "So now, with that, he's the only one left."

Clay explained Operation Big Hand was a CIA operation to smuggle drugs into the U.S. for money to fund the Contras fight in Nicaragua against the Sandinistas.

"That's absurd! The CIA is, well, almost a law enforcement agency, designed to protect America, not import drugs."

"Welcome to the world, Mary Beth. I thought the same thing a little over a month ago."

She said, "John Henry, I want to go see my doctor about some of these cuts and bruises and then I'll come back. What are we to do with all the bodies?"

Clay thought, I believe this woman has changed her thinking considerably. Before she wanted no one hurt, now she's nonchalantly talking about bodies we have to get rid of.

"When you come back after dark, I'll put them into their sedan and park it near the embassy. You can follow me and bring me back." He hesitated and said, "If you feel like it I'd like to have dinner with you."

"I look too bad to go out in public, but when I return I'll bring us some food. Do you like Chinese?"

145

"Yeah, I'll have the bodies stashed in the sedan by the time you get back."

She reached out and stroked his cheek where he had a horrible lump from his beating. "You need to have this looked at. You might have a chipped cheek bone."

After Mary Beth left, John Henry got dressed and went outside. The three bodies were stacked like cord-wood in front of the Agency sedan. He walked around the car and found he could get the bodies into the back seat from the left side of the car since the bushes would prevent anyone seeing him do it.

When Clay searched the bodies he found two of them had the little I.D. folders proclaiming them to be agents of the CIA. One of the men had no I.D. but lots of money, several thousand at least, which meant he was probably a cartel man the agency was using. He added the money to his growing bankroll as well as another Uzi and two more of the little .32 pistols.

He placed all the bodies across the back seat and shoved the legs in last. Then he slammed the car door shut.

Clay went back into the house, showered, shaved and doctored the worst of his cuts and bruises. His bathing got his slight thigh wound bleeding and he used a medicated powder from Karen's medicine cabinet to stop it.

He put on a change of clean civilian clothing and tucked one of the little pistols into a back pocket with a shirt tail out covering it. He sat down on the couch facing the front door, a pistol in his lap. Will the Striker come back? he wondered.

While he waited, Clay examined his growing feelings for Mary Beth. She had initially turned him off with her unrealistic view of the world—her belief that no one should die, even if they were evil. But now, she saw life as he did. He was powerfully attracted to her. It was even interfering with his concentration on finding the chief's killer. Could this be the woman for him? Only time would tell.

Three hours later the Striker had not shown up. Mary Beth came with Chinese food, and they ate; later she followed him to drop off the agency's car with its load of bodies.

NINETEEN

*"Inability to tell good from evil, is the greatest worry
of man's life."*
Cicero

The Deputy to the Director of Operations in Langley, Virginia, was being promoted. He was to assume full duties as the Director of Operations, Central Intelligence Agency.

He had just received a telephone call from Clayton Elliot, code named Big Hand. While the call was being switched to scramble he wondered again just what that operation was all about.

The voice came through the line with an echo meaning the call was being scrambled and the line was secure.

"Sir, this is "Big Hand." I have disastrous news. With the exception of one contract person all our Panama personnel are dead. The station chief, his assistant, and four operatives were killed yesterday, and today, along with three personnel on loan from a group of non-Americans involved in the operation. We have no assets in place except two flight crews from the Air Force."

"Good Lord, man. What happened down there?" The deputy asked with alarm.

"Sir, that son of a bitch friend of our traitor is constantly getting in our way. We thought we had him and an accomplice but he escaped and killed three operatives holding them captive.

"When the station chief of the Panama Section, and two of his men returned to interrogate the bastard, he killed all three of them." He added, "Only our contract operative, the Striker, escaped from the debacle. Operation Big Hand is now stalled.

"Elliot, just what is this Operation Big Hand?" the deputy asked.

There was a long silence on the line. Then Big Hand said, "Sir, if you don't know then I'm not at liberty to tell you."

The deputy director's anger boiled up but he contained it as well as he could. He said to "Big Hand," "As of 2400 hours tonight I will be the director of operations. I expect you at my office at 0900 hours tomorrow. Bring all your data on this operation for a full and comprehensive briefing to me. Is that understood?"

Elliot quickly answered, "Yes sir. You do understand my reluctance to discuss it with you not knowing your need to know?"

"Yes, Big Hand. I certainly do understand and I will make you properly aware of our chain of command at our meeting tomorrow. That is all." He hung up the phone.

Asshole, he thought. He quickly got up and strode in to the Director's office where his predecessor was packing his belongings, and in twenty minutes the retiring director had introduced him to the damnedest operation he had ever heard. It was completely outside the law and outside the parameters of the CIA's basic charter.

The entire operation had grown with no one person taking the responsibility for having started it. The new director, he thought, or the new director after midnight was putting a stop to the entire mess.

As of midnight the Striker was out and on his own. If this revenge-seeking ex-service man wanted to conduct a vendetta against the agency, that would be addressed at a later time; but if he was after the one who had killed his friend, then more power to him.

The new director of operations put in his call to Mr. Casey, the head of the CIA, to discuss ending this illegal operation.

TWENTY

"The only thing more dangerous than "Incoming"
enemy fire, is "Incoming" friendly fire."
Rule 25, Murphy's law of Combat

For three days John Henry Clay waited for the Striker. After three days he decided it was time to find the proof he was sure the chief had left for him in his safe-deposit box in Miami.

He told Mary Beth of his thinking and had her drive him out to the airport on the other side of Howard's Base operations.

As they pulled into the parking area Clay saw a fuel truck refueling a C-130. The tall enlisted man holding the fire extinguisher was Saul.

Clay kissed Mary Beth good-bye and promised to call her, then walked over to Saul and shook hands with him. He quickly told him what had happened including the fact that most of the "bad guys" were dead but that the Striker was still running around free.

Making conversation he asked where Saul's ship was going.

"To England Air Force Base in Louisiana, with a refueling stop in Miami. You heading that way, John Henry?"

"Yeah, Saul, but I don't want to get you in trouble."

"Bull shit, John Henry. Screw the director of operations. If you've got your passport and your nomex flight suit I'll just add you to our manifest and we're on our way."

Clay put on the flight suit and an hour later was on board the C-130. The aircraft commander, the same major who had taken in too many pisgah sours in Bolivia, nodded as he passed.

They landed in Miami International where the Customs people took the declaration forms that had already been prepared with Clay's name on one, counted noses, and departed.

Clay picked up his carry-on bag, shook hands with Saul, and wandered over to the terminal area. He found a rest room and quickly changed out of his nomex flight suit into casual civilian clothes.

He strolled out of the building to the taxi stand and, while waiting, analyzed the feelings he was getting. He felt the almost tropical heat that is standard for Miami, along with the fumes from too many cars, buses and taxis. He knew he was being watched and declined the first two taxis in line and got into the third one.

They headed for Fort Lauderdale as Clay had decided to put distance between himself and Miami, at least temporarily.

At a huge Holiday Inn in Fort Lauderdale, John Henry paid his thirty-five dollar fare plus a five dollar tip, and strolled into the motel heading for the registration desk. But he continued walking out the door to the pool area, then into a small bar.

He went to a semi-dark corner and sat down and waited. A barmaid came over and took his order. He nursed his drink for thirty minutes but only an older couple entered the bar during that entire time.

Feeling a little foolish, Clay settled his tab, paid a good tip, and asked if the bar had a street exit. He was told that it didn't but then was offered the employee exit, which he quickly accepted.

On the busy street Clay figured he was blending in but took a trip through a supermarket anyway, with a quick stop at their deli for a hot pastrami on rye bread.

He walked several blocks and came upon a motel spread out on half a city block. He registered as John Hay and paid cash for one night. In his room he shaved and showered and dressed in his cleanest dirty clothes, then left his room carrying his small bag, and walked to a used car lot about a block from his motel.

He made a deal with a hungry salesman and paid a thousand dollars for a twelve–year old Japanese import that he was familiar with, having owned one just like it. From the sound of the little four cylinder engine, the "rice-burner" car still had some life in it.

They slapped a temporary cardboard license in the rear window and Clay drove off looking for a gas station. A Hot Mart convenience store nearby served that purpose and he picked up a few quarts of 10W30 motor oil just in case the car was like his previous one.

He got back on I-95 and headed north at the posted speed limit. An hour and fifteen minutes later, just north of West Palm Beach, he got on the exit ramp and headed east toward the beaches. Several cars had followed him of which was not unusual, but the feeling of being followed was still riding him.

He slowed as if looking for a number. Sure enough two cars swung out as if to pass him, but both swung in and boxed him in on three sides and he skidded to a stop. Several men quickly jumped out of the cars. Most had Uzi's; and one had an old fashioned Thompson sub-machine gun.

They all pointed their weapons at John Henry. He slid the .32 caliber pistol he was holding under the seat. The other one was in his bag. Just maybe they would find it and be satisfied that he was unarmed.

He raised his hands and as one of them opened the door he slid out and stood there with seven armed men pointing automatic weapons at him. He felt as exposed as if he were in a crowded room and his pants had suddenly dropped to his ankles.

They patted him down. One searched his bag and pulled out one of their own .32s, and they appeared satisfied he was now harmless.

They put him in the back of one of their cars and one man got in his and the little four-car convoy pulled out and got back on I-95 south. They exited in West Palm Beach and pulled up to a posh resort-type motel. He was hustled inside, then into an elevator, which carried them to the third floor.

Clay felt he could have taken the four who were with him in the elevator but held off just to see what would happen.

They entered a room very near the elevator shaft and Clay was propelled to the front of a florid faced, middle-aged man with power written all over him. The agents who had brought him in were even standing at attention.

The man snapped out, "I'm Clayton Elliot, CIA Chief of Station Miami. You're the son of a bitch that's been killing my agents." With that little speech he back-handed Clay, whose earlier training in jiu-jit-su had conditioned him for such blows. His head turned and rode the blow on around. It hurt but there was not the steam a blow like that should normally bring. There must be something with the CIA big-wigs all wanting to slap their prisoners, Clay thought.

The man's swing had revealed a shoulder holster and a heavy caliber pistol under his jacket. Clay filed that knowledge away for the future.

The man glared at Clay and venom showed in his eyes. He said, "If it was up to me I'd kill you right now, but I've been directed otherwise. You are to be set free if you drop your vendetta against the agency and reveal nothing of what you think you know of Operation Big Hand. You'll be told where Holliman is and it's up to you if you want to go after him. He is no longer employed by the agency." He glared at Clay and said almost in a snarl. "Well, what's it to be?"

Clay said, "You're the one who ordered the chief's death, aren't you?"

The man looked startled for a second then replied, "He signed an agreement under penalty of death not to discuss anything with anyone."

"Maybe you're the one I should have been hunting."

Anger and frustration flashed over Elliot's face and he stepped forward and slapped Clay again, but this time when Clay rode with the slap his hand reached up and yanked the big .45 caliber automatic from under the man's jacket. John Henry didn't know whether the man carried it with a round in the chamber or not so he yanked the receiver at the top of the pistol to the rear and the bolt went forward sliding a round in the chamber and cocking it at the same time for firing.

He thumbed the safety down. The big pistol was loaded, hammer back and ready to fire.

He pulled Elliot around and put the big pistol to his forehead. He looked at the four very surprised agents, each in varying stages of reaching for their weapons.

He ordered, "One at a time, you first" and he motioned to the one whose hand was completely out of sight under his jacket. "Bring it out with two fingers. If I see three fingers on it I blow this guy away then try for you next."

The man did as he was told. Clay was surprised when the weapon he pulled turned out to be a Uzi sub-machine gun. The other three were also carrying Uzi's and Clay knew they had developed a holster or some means to carry them out of sight.

Clay had them all step back from the weapons that now lay on a small coffee table. "Now, the pistols. Step up one at time and pull them out."

No one moved so Clay shoved the Miami Station Chief to one side and stepped toward them ordering them to turn around as he did. "I'm going to search you all, one at at time. When I feel a weapon I put a .45 hole in that man's head. Are we ready?"

The tallest of the four said, "Wait a minute, mister. I have another weapon."

Clay pointed the big pistol at him and said, "Okay with two fingers pull it out." The man did and Clay stepped up behind him and took the small Beretta from his two fingers.

He stepped back and asked, "Any more weapons, amigos?"

When Clay finally had them all disarmed, he stood slightly behind Elliot, the Miami Station Chief.

Clay said, "Listen up, all of you. I'm going to make a little speech and it might mean your life if you aren't paying attention. The CIA has been smuggling drugs into this country for the Medallin Cartel in Buga, Columbia. It was done for money. Millions and millions of dollars. A good friend of mine kept records and saved absolute proof of everything. They found out he had discussed it with me and they executed him, even though he had worked for the agency for over twenty-five years. It was a contract killer they used and the bastard has been running away from me just about all over South America."

"Now," he went on, "you know what kind of outfit you're working for. They preyed on addicts, men, women and children of our own country for money. They're saying now they want me to quit. I will quit if the agency gets out of the drug smuggling business and leaves me completely alone."

Clay ended his little speech with, "Mr. Elliot, tell them what I can do, just in case you people are tempted to come after me."

Elliot was not liking Clay's "speech" at all but he gave the facts of Clay's military record, his awards and decorations, his weapon's qualifications, and ended it with, "He's killed eleven agents and eight contract people and is extremely dangerous. But our higher ups want to stop this right now so we'll keep our end of the bargain. The operation is over and we don't want to lose any other people or get a bad press because of whatever he thinks he can prove. The man he's after is Carl Holliman, code name Striker, who had been discharged from the agency. As of four PM yesterday he was in Miami, staying at the El Juban motel just outside Little Havana. We know nothing of his plans."

He glared at Clay and his anger was riding him hard. "As I've said, upstairs wants it all to end, but if it was left to me you wouldn't last a day, you son of a bitch."

Clay grinned and to tweak him a little more said, "You think your agents will ever have any respect for you after today? Slapping a man around when he's unarmed and helpless? That's not classy, at all, Elliot."

The reaction from Elliot was more glares so John Henry walked to the coffee table, lay down the big .45 and picked up a Uzi, and .32 and said to the man who had given it up, "Hand me the silencer for this thing, please."

The man reached into his inside coat pocket with Clay's own pistol following his movements. He handed over the screw on, baffle-nose silencer and Clay screwed it on, watching the five of them all the while.

He turned to Elliot and said, "The deal's on amigo, but I think you might be feeling lucky sometime off in the future and then I'll have the great pleasure of killing you."

He added, "I'm walking out the door and I hope you know your best choice is to stop it right here." With that, Clay, weapons ready, walked out the door.

He expected a guard outside but the hallway was empty. He passed the elevator and entered the stairwell, stuffing his Uzi in the small of his back and holding it there by his belt.

He carried the .32 in his right hand with the safety off. At the ground floor he exited the stairwell and turned to the street.

The guys were professionals and they were head and shoulders better than those he had faced in South America. But, when he exited the luxury motel he spotted all three agents having a quiet conversation next to his newly purchased "rice burner."

He recalled from his time in combat how even the best of his troops tended to gather together, and no matter how many times he screamed "one round will get you all" they would continue to do it just like these agents.

He moved their way and was only four or five steps from them when one noticed him. All three moved their hands to their jackets but Clay raised the .32. They froze. Then all dropped their hands.

Clay moved to his car and said, "Keys?" The beefy one pulled the keys with the used car lot tag still attached to them, and held them out to Clay.

John Henry stepped back, pointing the pistol at him and said in a low voice, "Pitch them gently or I'll shoot you."

The man hesitated just slightly then pitched the keys to Clay who plucked them out of the air with his left hand.

Clay said, "Your boss, Mr. Elliot, set me free. He told me that if I let you guys alone you would leave me alone. Don't do something stupid and mess up our deal."

He backed to the little used car, opened the door and slid in, all in one motion with the pistol pointed at the three agents the entire time. He switched the pistol to his left hand, put the key in with his right and started the car.

Clay shut the door and drove off, not stomping the accelerator like he wanted to. He could see the three agents just standing there as he turned off at the first corner.

He went back to I-95 and headed south, which was a change of plans as he had intended to come home to Bal Cove, to pick up the safe-deposit box key and the authorization letter to the bank in Miami. With his agreement with Elliot of the CIA there was no need to get the materials now, so his main priority was the Striker.

Elliot had said he was no longer connected to the CIA and also said as of four PM yesterday the man was at the El Juban motel just at the edge of the section of Miami called Little Havana.

Clay had a friend with a Cuban restaurant right in Little Havana. His name was Ramon Rodrigues, but when he was in the forces with Clay everyone called him Chico, probably after the pro golfer named Chi Chi.

Chico had gotten tired of the killing, the misdirection of the war and the real lack of promotion opportunities in Special Forces. He was also one helluva cook, with the ability to take a can of Spam and make a feast fit for a king.

Clay knew Chico had contacts and information on just about everybody and every thing going on in Miami. It was through Chico that Clay had gotten the bodyguarding job that had taken him to South America in the first place.

His first move then, was to return to Miami and talk to Chico. He had also been a good friend of the chief and often in "Nam" would have the chief bring in special spices and condiments so he could work his culinary wonders.

Clay spent the night in his motel room in Fort Lauderdale and his drive down I-95 and into Miami proper the next evening was uneventful. He pulled into the parking lot of the *Roja Asno* restaurant after turning west off I-95. His drive there had taken him past an old garage with about a half block under a roof and there must have been seventy-five to a hundred Cuban people, sitting on benches, milling around, talking, and playing dominoes. All seemed to be waiting for something to happen in their homeland.

Clay wondered how many of the thousands of Cuban families would return if something should happen to Castro.

He entered the restaurant and caught the eye of a man who motioned toward one of the small dining rooms with his chin. Clay went into it and took a seat in a corner booth where he could watch the front as well as a side doorway leading into another dining room.

In about two minutes Chico came in, made about four stops along the way, slapping the backs of some of his patrons, very formal with others, bowing and hand shaking, then he was in front of Clay.

Clay rose. They clasped hands and Chico said, "John Henry, how goes the chase?" and Clay knew that he knew the chief was dead and that Clay was after his killer. That

Chico knew was no surprise to Clay. He didn't even wonder who had given him the information.

Clay said, "Not so well, amigo. The bastard is quick on his feet. As of yesterday he was at the El Juban motel. I thought you might be able to check on it for me."

"Describe the bastardo, mi amigo, and the name he goes by if you know it."

Clay gave him Holliman's name and a quick description, including the fact the man was mean, quick and unstable.

Chico sat there a minute looking at Clay's black and blue features and the many bruises, and finally he said, "If he is the one that did this to you," and he waved to Clay's face, "then he is too formidable for my poor compadres."

Clay laughed but stopped when he saw Chico's serious face. "Amigo, the *lubio bastardo* did this, but my hands were cuffed behind me and he had two others to help him. I killed the two but he fled. Then I killed three others who came to help him. Do you perhaps think I am too *viejo*?"

Chico said, "John Henry, I meant no disrespect for it is common knowledge in the forces that you had no peer, in fighting or figuring, but never have I seen so many cuts and bruises on one face." He gave a short laugh and went on, "Mahoney in Seventh Group thought he was the toughest but we could never get him to come to the ring and meet you. I, myself, saw him fight and he was very strong, and I think maybe he could stand with you for maybe one round, but your quickness and strength would make it a short round."

"Thank you, Chico, I think! But I do not want help with the Striker. I just want to locate him without giving away my presence by marching in to the motel desk, *Comprend*?"

"Si, John Henry. *Uno momento* please. I will return."

The waiter brought several dishes and put them in front of Clay and the aroma of the food awoke the hunger and he fell to eating. As soon as he finished one dish something equally delicious would be set before him.

He washed it all down with a rose blush wine that was in a class all by itself.

When Chico returned, he observed the empty dishes and said, "Never, John Henry, have I felt that anyone appreciates my food more than you."

Clay grinned at him and said, "I was hooked on your food from the time you fixed that four foot gecko lizard for us in Cambodia."

Chico laughed and said, "Those *muy hombres* would have eaten it alive and kicking if I had not been there to cook it."

His face become serious and Chico said, "John Henry, this one is sicko in the head. He is in room twenty four of the El Juban motel. He prowls the streets and bars for low-class whores and takes them, one, two or three at a time to his room. He beats them and does unspeakable things to them, and he shares his white powder with them."

He went on, "He also goes to the better places. Last night he was seen at the Copacabana supper club in Coral Gables. He picked up a young university coed and they went to a place near the university where they had several drinks."

"When they returned to the parking lot the man got violent and severely beat the young girl. One of my young men tells me there was a killing of another young coed about a week ago where the assailant used his fists and feet to beat her to death. The Miami Police Department is keeping it "under wraps" but they want to find the man as the beatings were similar, except the second girl was lucky and survived.

162

"A few days ago he entered an adult book store in south Miami on U.S. 1, that specializes in toys for the gay population. He spent a few hours watching their dirty movies which I've been told are very dirty."

"Chico, you amaze me. How did you find out so much in such a short time?"

"John Henry, Little Havana is a small *barrio* and any one who is a stranger is watched. Only after many, many months, can one blend in here. I remember our military intelligence training and, how do you say it? I have a "network" of informers."

"Okay, Chico, I'm a believer, but does your intel network know where the Striker is now?"

"Your killer friend is having an early dinner at this very minute at a posh supper club in Miami Beach. His guest, or host, is Clayton Elliot, Miami CIA Station Chief."

"Why, that dirty, rotten asshole!" Clay burst out. "The CIA is supposed to be out of this. I ought to put him on my list of eliminations, then go shorten it by one tonight."

"Who, John Henry? The CIA man or the Striker?"

"That damn CIA station chief. He was ordered out of this so why is he meeting with an ex-contract killer? Unless he's not an "ex" contract killer. Amigo, how long would it take me to get over to the beach? To this place where they're meeting?"

It would take you forty-five minutes to an hour. But with me to take you there, maybe fifteen minutes. Shall we go?"

Chico ran red lights and went at speeds forty to fifty miles per hour over the limits. Twice policemen in their prowl cars saw them and averted their eyes. Chico obviously enjoyed a special status. They crossed into Miami Beach over the Venetian Isle toll road causeway.

They pulled into the Bamboo Club parking lot and since the club required coat and tie Chico produced a sports jacket and a snap-on tie. Clay donned the extra clothes then transferred the .32 pistol to the small of his back under the jacket.

Chico said he would wait. Clay entered the fancy establishment and spotted the two, heads together in deep conversation, in a booth large enough for a party of five or six.

As luck would have it a party of two couples moved that way in front of Clay, who ignored the maitre-d's urgent waving of hands.

As he neared the table Clay's right hand went under his borrowed jacket and as he sat down at the table with the CIA Station Chief and the Striker he let them see the pistol before he put it under the table out of sight.

Elliot quickly looked at another table where two young, burly, well-dressed men sat. Both began rising from their seats.

Clay said, "You're dead meat if they come over, asshole." He was looking at the CIA Station Chief and his anger was making his look a glare.

A quick wave of the hand from Elliot and both men sat back down at their table. John Henry turned his eyes to Holliman and almost snarled, "The last woman lived, you damned sadistic bastard. But that's okay, for you're not long for this world."

Holliman sucked air noisily and his eyes shifted back and forth as if he were looking for a way out. Clay could feel the man's shock and fear and he knew only a part of it was from Clay's revelation that he knew about the killing of one coed and the severe beating of another. The rest of it was his deep fear of Clay. He had come up lacking each time they had met, and he was deeply effected by it.

John Henry wanted desperately to end it all right there, and blow both of these insensitive bastards away. They were in a crowded public place, however, and innocent civilians would inevitably be killed in a firefight.

Gritting his teeth he said to Elliot, "So our deal is off, asshole?"

Elliot answered, "No, I was simply explaining to Mr. Holliman that his employment is ended. Isn't that right, Mr. Holliman?" He was sweating although they were sitting in chilled air conditioned air."

Holliman hurriedly confirmed that he no longer worked for the agency and Clay could see the sudden hope on his face that maybe Clay was going to let him live. But those hopes were dashed when Clay looked him in the eye and said, "You have two hours, Holliman. Then I'm coming to kill you." With that Clay stood up and left the crowded restaurant.

TWENTY-ONE

"When all else is equal, the side with the simplest
uniforms win!"
Rule 30, Murphy's law of Combat

Clay returned to Chico's car and they returned to Little
Havana at a more sedate speed. John Henry told Chico
what had happened and Chico agreed that too many innocent lives were at stake so he had done the right thing by
holding off killing the Striker then and there.

Back at the *Rojo Asno* Chico and Clay enjoyed a drink
of Chico's fine wine and they reminisced. Clay's attempts
to pay his dinner tab afterwards failed as Chico was firm
in his refusal to accept money from Clay.

He told Clay to take his meals there and he would
provide intelligence on the Striker's movements. They
shook hands and Clay left.

For three days John Henry watched the motel where
the Striker had stayed, to no avail. None of Chico's sources
had seen the man. Chico even had several of his airport
contacts check out the flight manifests for air lines serving
South America. There was not a trace of the man. It was if
he had gone into a hole in the ground and gotten covered up.

On the fourth day Clay went to the bank to check the chief's safe deposit box. As he had guessed it contained proof that the CIA had ran drugs into Los Angeles for the Medelin Cartel.

There were photographs of CIA personnel, their names entered on each photo, C-130 aircraft tail numbers and the crews helping "civilians." A dozen or more pictures showed trucks, their license tags in full view, being loaded. The years on the license tags indicated at least three different years.

There was a lot of cash, mostly in ten thousand dollar bundles, and the chief's last will and testament. Clay's quick glance revealed the bulk of his estate was to go to his finance Karen Harper. There were bequests to Clay and Robert Whipple, and two others Clay did not know, in the amount of one hundred thousand dollars each. Clay was named executor.

A letter of instructions to the executor was to the effect that the cash was to be distributed equally between the four if there was more than the four hundred thousand dollars in his box. The chief also owned lot of stock and high interest corporate bonds. Clay was not surprised to find that the Chief had been a wealthy man.

On the fifth day Chico called Clay, "I do not know if it means anything but one of the baggage handlers at the airport reported a military aircraft, a C-130, refueled there the day before yesterday. He reports that a big man with almost blond hair boarded. He checked just today and found it was manifested to Howard AFB, Panama."

"Chico, I'll bet that's it! I'll call for a reservation to Panama on the next available flight this after. . . ." But Chico broke in, "You have reservation on Pan Am for two thirty, P.M. today." He laughed and said, "Pay and pick up ticket at the counter."

"Amigo, you are very efficient. I do thank you, Chico."

"Just off that asshole that did the chief."

When Clay hung up he placed a call to Mary Beth Coleman at the dependents school in Panama, leaving word for her to call him as soon as possible, adding, "This is crucial and could be a matter of life or death."

In less than fifteen minutes a breathless Mary Beth was on the line. "Oh, John Henry. I was going to call you today, cause I wasn't able to get through to you last night. Yesterday I thought I saw that man you've been chasing. He was across from the Admin Building of the school and he was definitely watching the school buildings. I was frightened, so I slipped out and went home with a friend. There was no answer when I called you last night."

"Baby, I was out till real late trying to find him. I just got word today that he flew out of Miami day before yesterday. I'm manifested on the Pan-Am flight to Panama today and should be getting in there at six-thirty this evening. Be real careful, honey, but see if you can meet me at the air terminal. Do you think you can do it without him seeing you?"

"He's seen my car and knows it, but I can leave my car at the school and have a girl friend drive me out there."

"All right, baby. Bring one of the little pistols with the silencer on it and a couple of extra magazines of ammunition, from that stash I left with you."

"Okay. Tell me, have you missed me a little since you've been gone?"

"Not a little, Mary Beth, a whole lot. In fact, I want to talk to you about your getting out of your contract down there. I'd sort of like to have you around me all the time."

"John Henry, are you proposing? and over the phone at that?"

"Yes, Mary Beth. I believe I am."

She giggled and said, "I'm accepting and you'd better not be teasing me."

"No teasing, Mary Beth. I'm as serious as a heart attack. I love you." He added, "I'll see you this evening. Be careful."

That afternoon at 1830 hours or 6:30 PM, the Pan Am flight jet landed in Panama. Clay hurried out of the air terminal and spotted Mary Beth and another American young woman.

He threw his arms around her and they kissed passionately until finally Mary Beth squirmed free and said, "John Henry, there's people around."

Then she introduced him to the school teacher with her and John Henry said all the polite things, and they picked up his bag and walked to a green, ugly, Mazda car. But despite the appearance it started and hummed like a new sewing machine.

The young woman Mary Beth had introduced as Dorothy something-or-another, was a very good driver. She wasn't reckless but she entered the holes in the traffic with finesse.

In the car Mary Beth pressed a paper bag into his hand and he causally slipped bag, pistol and all into his right side jacket pocket.

Dorothy drove them to Mary Beth's car. The women hugged good by and John Henry mumbled, "So good to meetcha," and she drove off.

Clay went over the car: under the hood, in the trunk, on the manifold and in the tail pipe. There were no explosive devices anywhere about the car so they got in and drove to Mary Beth's little house.

Clay searched it, inside and out, and found nothing. He had Mary Beth turn lights on and he slipped out the back and circled the house. If the Striker was there he was certainly well hidden.

After an hour of waiting and watching he decided Holliman was somewhere else, and he re-entered the house.

Mary Beth took food from her small freezer and in less than an hour they were enjoying a good meal. Clay thought to himself, Thank the Lord she can cook, for his ex-wife could not boil water without burning it.

They got little rest and Clay told himself again how lucky he was, for they were ideally suited for each other, and enjoyed all the aspects of their love making.

The next day, Friday, Clay dropped Mary Beth off at the school. He drove around for a while then walked back, hoping to catch the Striker watching the school.

Their arrangement was for him to pick her up at 1500 hours, or three o'clock that afternoon. At 3:30 Clay locked the little car and went in to the Administration Office where he was told Mary Beth had had an emergency and had left at lunch time.

No one saw who she left with except Dorothy, who had just come by and saw him in the office. She had not talked to Mary Beth but saw her get into a blue sedan, like the military sedans. It headed southeast, which is nothing but jungle unless they turned off somewhere in another direction.

Clay immediately thanked them all and ran to Mary Beth's little car. As he sped through intersections and stop signs at top speeds he fumed at the plain evidence that the agency was still giving the Striker support in his effort to cause Clay problems and to eventually do him in and thereby escape blame for murdering the chief.

John Henry knew he could not catch up with one of the CIA's big sedans but he wanted to be as close as possible when the Striker got to where he was going.

About twenty miles down the road with heavy jungle on both sides and no signs of human habitation except for the macadam road itself, Clay almost sped past the blue sedan, pulled into a hole in the jungle.

He backed up and into the hole next to the sedan and got out, his .32 out, round in the chamber, and ready.

A beaten down path went north through the heavy jungle growth and Clay followed it, very sense alert and his nerves tingling. He could feel the old adrenaline flowing as it did back in 'nam when he was leading a patrol to meet the enemy.

His nose was assailed by the heavy, cloying aroma of the verdant jungle growth. There was also the feral smell of the animal life of the jungle, and Clay's heightened sense of awareness made him note the silence of the normally raucous sounds of the jungle.

This could mean, his own movement through the thick growth was disturbing the wildlife activity, or that the previous intrusion by the Striker and his prisoner, Mary Beth, had caused it.

Some five hundred yards through the jungle growth he suddenly came upon a cabin, practically overtaken by vines and jungle growth.

He took the time to circle and examine the small, still visible clearing around the small cabin.

John Henry was sure this was Holliman's jungle hideout and he could almost feel the traps and snares set for him.

He called upon his long years of combat experience and closed on the cabin. He was almost sniffing for the expected trip wires, or treadles to trigger explosive devices, and other little goodies Clay knew Holliman was capable of installing.

Clay found only one trip wire that activated a warning device: tin cans with loose nails in them that rattled when the wire was touched.

He tried the door, It was locked so he went around the little cabin checking for unlocked windows. There were no open ones and Clay moved away from the cabin to consider everything.

The situation was one of two things. Either the Striker knew Clay would be able to follow and was therefore inside waiting, or he believed Clay could not or had not followed, and he was at that moment inside ravishing the sweet Mary Beth.

This thought straightened Clay up. He got a hold of himself and made his decision. He would go in.

The door appeared solid and all the windows were awning types except for the one facing him from where he crouched. He thought about it a second, checked his pistol, then lunged into a run. He covered his face and head with his arms, and dived through the window, rolling to the far wall, at the same time swinging the little .32 from side to side.

The room was empty but the Striker appeared at the door on his left and blasted two shots with his .32, then bolted as Clay's own .32 pecked holes in the door frame near him.

All shots missed their target. John Henry jumped to his feet but as he ran to the doorway, he could hear the Striker's feet pounding on the wooden floor.

He charged into the front room of the little cabin and got just a glimpse as Holliman exited hurriedly from the cabin through the previously locked front door.

Clay's one shot smacked into the closing door, and he ran to it, threw it open and emptied the remaining eight rounds in the little pistol at the Striker, who was entering the jungle some forty yards away, at a dead run.

Clay pulled the empty magazine from the pistol and inserted a full one, then turned to check the house for Mary Beth.

He entered the third room which was fixed like a torture dungeon. There were no windows and the only light came from the open door. There were iron rings mounted on the walls, an iron maiden torture device, and other chains and whips around the wall.

Mary Beth was chained to the wall, her skirt and blouse in disarray, with the blouse practically torn off her. Her eyes were wide open showing the whites, and she appeared to be almost in a state of shock.

Clay walked over to her and said, "Mary Beth, if you like this stuff so much we'll have to have one room decorated like this in our house."

Her "in shock" look disappeared and she said, "Damn you, John Henry, when are you gonna kill that bastard and end this crap?"

He said, "I'm trying real hard, baby. Now how do I get you out of these chains?"

She nodded to a shelf where there were about a dozen keys on a ring, one apparently for every device in the torture room.

He quickly found the right key and released Mary Beth and told her he was going after the Striker and that she should stay there or go to the car.

She replied, "No way, John Henry. I go where you go. I want to see him dead."

"Okay, Mary Beth." In reality he had no choice for Holliman could circle around and return to the cabin or his sedan.

They entered the jungle by a small path where the Striker had entered. Clay had Mary Beth stay behind him and he made good time, his eyes searching the path and bushes along side for signs of his quarry.

He found a foot print here and there where the ground was soft, and in one place found the Strikers two foot prints together as he had stopped and had looked behind him.

The hair stood up on the back of Clay's neck as he heard the now familiar coughing snarl of a jaguar. This was a big one, the cough deep with menace.

He continued to follow the path for about thirty minutes then realized the throaty cough of the big jaguar was moving ahead of him, and he wondered if it was between him and the Striker.

Ten minutes later the path entered a soft area of ground, and there were the pug marks, or the paw prints of a large jaguar.

It was a giant with large foot prints pressed deep in the soft ground, but, with a shock, Clay realized there were no foot prints of the Striker.

Clay motioned Mary Beth to hold up and his eyes searched the surrounding jungle and trees, trying to spot Holliman if he had stopped to try an ambush.

He crept quietly back to Mary Beth and pushed her down to the floor of the jungle. He mouthed to her, "Stay here," then he slid back along the trail they had been following and came to the turn where Clay had last remembered seeing the Striker's tracks.

He got down close to the ground and crawled along and found where the Striker had stepped off the trail into sparse jungle on the right hand side of the path.

Clay visually searched the trees, bushes and anything in sight but saw nothing but Holliman's trail leading off to the south.

He raised up and signaled Mary Beth to come on to him. When she got there he whispered to her, "I don't know whether the big cat caused him to leave the trail, or whether it's a short cut, but I don't see how he can ambush us in this stuff, so we'll keep on after him."

It was slow going as Clay had to be alert for an ambush and he took no chances with Mary Beth along.

A half hour later Clay had followed Holliman's trail back upon the beaten path again. In about fifteen minutes of cautious walking in some more soft ground, Clay found the Striker's tracks and behind them, the track of the big jaguar.

There was no doubt now. The big cat was behind Holliman and was actually stepping in his foot prints as he hurried on. The jaguar gave every indication that he was stalking Holliman and Clay had to wonder now if the man knew it.

They speeded up their pace with both sets of tracks in front of them. By now the distance between the cat's tracks had lengthened quite a bit, telling Clay the jaguar was now running.

They both suddenly froze as a terrified scream sounded and was cut off. They heard a single shot and then the big animal snarled. It was the first sound the cat had made since it had begun stalking the unfortunate Holliman.

Clay whispered to Mary Beth, "Stay here, I'll go check it out," but she was shaking her head so he turned and hurriedly moved down the trail with Mary Beth right at his heels.

Clay and Mary Beth rounded a bend in the trail and there they were: Holliman, his body torn almost to rags and the big jaguar crouched over him, his bright yellow eyes glaring at them.

Clay had his pistol out and pointed at the cat, praying for a good shot if the big animal sprang. As he took several cautious steps toward the beast and the Striker's body, he could smell the fresh blood.

The jaguar watched Clay advance, his long tail swinging from side to side, his baleful yellow eyes glittering with rage.

At last the animal backed off the body and with every step Clay took his pistol out and at the ready, the big cat gave ground until it was almost at another bend in the trail and Clay was over the body.

His vision was brutally clear. Clay knew there were few things in a soldier's life so clear, so poignant as the sharply etched actions of his first battle. John Henry had the same feelings as he stood over the torn body of the chief's killer. He had known it from the time he had seen the tracks of the giant jaguar.

He very slowly sank to his knees and searched the dead Striker's pockets, finding the keys to the big sedan and quite a bit of American money.

He shoved it all in his pockets, keeping eye contact all the time with the giant cat, who was crouched there on the path, his tail whipping from side to side.

Clay pulled out his knife and with two quick strokes he cut Holliman's ears off and stuffed them into his pocket, noting there was practically no blood.

Clay stood up and the big animal tensed, then Clay stepped back and the jaguar stepped forward. This went on a step at a time until finally Clay was back with Mary Beth and the big cat was again over Holliman's body.

Perhaps some purists would say that allowing the big cat to eat Holliman would endanger innocent villagers by allowing the cat to taste human flesh. They would think that Clay should have done something about it, but with just a .32 caliber pistol, two of them now, Clay believed the fight would be unequal, so he begged off and left the spoils to the victor.

He and Mary Beth, once out of sight of the big cat, loped down the trail, finally getting back to Holliman's jungle cabin.

There was only one more coughing snarl from the big Jaguar, as if to say, "Thank you, my brother. I will see to the body."

Clay searched the cabin, not really knowing what he was looking for. What he found almost turned his stomach for the Striker liked to photograph all he had done to at least thirty different girls and women.

He had used the timer on his camera and was in most of the pictures, his face usually flushed with bestial, sexual urges. Clay took the expensive camera off its tripod and smashed it.

This probably was not the time to be thinking of revenge against the CIA, but Clay knew that at least Clayton Elliot had continued to assist the Striker, and for that he would have to suffer.

But why kill him now? If there was a chance he could keep peace with the agency, maybe that was the way to go. He would, however, send Elliot the Striker's ears and his collection or photos to show him the type of man they had been using.

Clay made a pile of papers and with a last look around, lit them. Before they reached the car flames were already breaking through the roof. The black clouds being pushed to the sky appeared evil and Clay knew it wasn't only the chief who had been avenged.

TWENTY-TWO

"To everything there is a season, and a time to every purpose under the heavens. A time to be born, and a time to die, a time to plant, and a time to reap, a time to kill and a time to heal."
Ecclesiastes, 1–8

Time had been good for Clay and Mary Beth in the seven years since the jaguar killed the Striker. They had married about two weeks later, and returned to the states. In the intervening years they had brought two children into the world, a boy and a girl.

Clay had applied for a position on the Bal Cove Police Department, and had been sponsored by them for acceptance into the Police Academy in Tampa, although he had to pay the fee himself.

He graduated from the academy and was taken on by the police department as a rookie officer. In two years he succeeded the retiring Chief of Police. The seven–man force acknowledged Clay was the man for the job and the city council agreed.

Now, five years later, Bal Cove was practically crime free with only some small time juvenile thieves to upset the smooth running township.

Bal Cove was essentially a working class town with most of the people employed in the nearby tourist and retirement communities along the Gold Coast.

Clay was taking part in an investigation of an attempted extortion of one of the few retired rich residents of Bal Cover.

The delivery of the money being extorted had been agreed upon and Clay was atop the highest building in Bal Cove. From the four-story building top Clay could look down on most of the little town where he was Chief of Police.

The point for the "drop" of the money was in clear view of the waiting police chief and other police officers positioned to see whoever picked up the money, and other police officers who could follow their escape route whenever the extortionists went. Then there were two police cars positioned to make the stop, again, regardless of the escape route taken.

The dull, leaden sky indicated something coming and Clay looked out to the western horizon and saw dark, mountainous thunder heads, with frequent flashes of heat lightening flickering across the dark masses off in the distance.

He knew the big lake was that way about forty miles. Lake Okeechobee was one of the largest lakes in the United States, and she was a killer.

It was a shallow lake and just a little wind could whip up boat-destroying waves. In 1928 she came out of the banks and when she receded she left hundreds dead and thousands of houses destroyed.

The Corps of Army Engineers bulldozed and concreted huge dikes around to contain her, but Clay had the feeling the huge, monster lake was just biding her time.

Clay continued to observe the "drop" site and came full alert as he spotted a very suspicious car. It was a large, white awfully familiar sedan and alarm bells started going off in his head as he realized the sedan was the type the CIA and the military purchased.

When the car circled the block and headed back to the west Clay got a look at the occupants. They were two men, youngish and smooth shaven, both in CIA "work clothes" that is, business suits and conservative ties.

It could be coincidence, but to someone like Clay there were very few "coincidences" in life.

Clay had felt since that time seven years ago when he had packaged up Holliman's ears and his large collection of photos of the women he had tortured and killed, and mailed them to Clayton Elliot, the Miami CIA Station Chief, that the matter was not settled. The CIA was too big and powerful and Clayton Elliot was one to carry a grudge.

Those horrible photos would convince anyone that Holliman was a murdering, sexual deviate, and they could have probably cleared up some old murders and disappearances in Miami and Panama, as not all of the pictures had been taken in the Striker's hideaway.

Clay was so engrossed wondering what possible reason two CIA field operatives would have to be in his town, with no courtesy visit or notification to the local authorities as was required by law, that he almost failed to see a tall, skinny man with a pony tail of scraggly hair and horn rimmed glasses, make the pickup.

He triggered the mike and said, "All units, stand by. Pickup made by older teenager, with a pony tail and tinted glasses. "He's six foot three or four inches and thin. He's walking east and seems to be waiting to be picked up." Adams, do you have him in sight?"

"Roger, Chief. The perp is a stranger to me and I've been around for over thirty years. I have him in sight. Do we grab him?"

He keyed the mic and said, gently, "Let's hold off grabbing him so we can get the rest of the gang."

Since the pickup man was under surveillance by his people Clay was starting to leave the roof of the building, when he saw a car pull around a nearby corner and slowly coast up to the walking pickup man.

The man opened the car door, leaned forward and kissed the driver of the car as he settled into the seat beside her.

Clay keyed his mic again and said, "Okay, close in and apprehend them. I believe we have the whole gang," and he laughed.

Clay drove to the street where the suspects had been stopped.

Adams met him as he stepped from his car. "Chief, I do believe the 'doee' is the 'doer.'

Trying not to laugh in Adam's earnest face Clay said, "Was the woman related to the extortion victim?"

"Yes sir. She's his grand daughter and I believe I saw her at his house when he told us about the threat."

"Okay Adams, take them to the jail, fingerprint them and book them for attempted extortion before I get there and call him on it."

"Yes sir." Adams left and Clay walked slowly back to his car. What should he do about the agency boys? Should he give them the first shot, or act now before they got the feel of the place?

He knew he had only the one option. They were after him and they were supremely confident they could take the "old" forty-seven-year-old man. The fact they were here meant Clayton Elliot had become more powerful or his higher ups had removed the screen protecting Clay.

At the police station both the suspects were booked, fingerprinted, and put into holding cells.

Clay went into his little office and closed the door then called the extortionist's target. He reported they had apprehended a young couple and recovered the money.

He intentionally did not tell him it was his grand daughter. She could break the news to him later and maybe the little bit of extra time in the slammer might do her good.

When he finished talking he placed a call to Chico in Miami at the *Roja Asno* restaurant. Chico came on the phone almost immediately and they passed pleasantries a few minutes, then Clay asked, "Amigo, how good is your intelligence net?"

"How do you mean, John Henry?"

"I need to know if Clayton Elliot is still the Station Chief in Miami. Can you find out?"

"John Henry, you surprise me. You yourself, are in the business and yet you do not know that Mr. Casey, the head of the Agency, has died and everyone apparently was moved up. Clayton Elliot is now the new Director of CIA Operations. Does this info help you, John Henry?"

"Sure does, Chico. It clarifies things and I do appreciate it."

"Okay then, mighty police chief, why don't you bring the beautiful Mary Beth to my place for a fine Spanish meal?"

"I'll do that, mi amigo. I may be busy for a couple weeks, but after that, okay?"

"I will be preparing my little restaurant for her visit."

"Okay Chico, I will call," and he hung up the phone.

News Item:
West Palm Beach, Florida
August 24th.

Rescue workers today pulled a white, four-door sedan from the deep canal along Interstate 95, just west of
West Palm Beach.

Two bodies were inside, Medical personnel on the
scene believe they drowned when their car left the Interstate at a high rate of speed the night before. It is suspected that it was a alcohol related incident.

Authorities on the scene refused to divulge the iden-
tities until next of kin are notified. It was reported, however, that both men were federal government employees.
End Item.

Three days prior before the sedan was found John
Henry told Mary Beth he had to take a few days off and
do some fishing.

"Where are you going? she asked, for she knew he had
not really gotten into salt water fishing.

"I think I'll go over to the lake and fish with Indian
Joe for a few days."

Mary Beth had met Indian Joe, a man who had waist-
length hair, a hook nose and a swarthy complexion. He
wore beads, cowboy clothes, and a lot of turquoise jewelry.

When he was a master sergeant in Clay's B Team there
was not a better fighting man anywhere, and he never said
he was an Indian.

Clay learned later that Joe had quit the Forces, served
out his enlistment period and gotten out of the service.

Joe had picked up a fifty percent disability for some
of his numerous wounds, so now he played as an Indian,
fished in Okeechobee, drank and chased women.

Clay thought Indian Joe was about ten years older than himself but wasn't sure for, except for the gray hair, he was youthful in his appearance and smooth as oil in his movements.

Clay didn't call first to tell Joe he was coming over for one simple reason: Joe had no phone and refused to put one in. His philosophy was, if it was so important for someone to talk to him they should come see him and talk in person.

Clay had no problem pin-pointing his agency adversaries. They were registered in Fort Lauderdale in the same motel their boss, Clayton Elliot, had used to work his deal with Clay, seven years earlier.

Clay left immediately for Okeechobee and was there in about an hour. He pulled up to Joe's ramshackle hootch. Joe wasn't there, so Clay walked around to the back. Joe's boat wasn't at his dock either, so Clay sat down in the covered area of the boat-house to wait.

Clay was good at waiting. He had stayed on some twiggys, or ambushes, for days at a time in 'nam. He made himself comfortable on a pine wooden bench and for about three hours he did not move except to check his watch.

There was a whining "putt-putt" of a very old outboard motor, and Joe came around a bend of the canal and smoothly guided the big "Jon boat" into the slip, and Clay pitched him one of the several tie ropes.

After Joe secured the boat and removed five or six large black bass, he and Clay shook hands and Joe said, "John Henry, what brings you over here? I know you're not wanting to go fishing, right?"

Let's go inside, Joe. I need to talk to you and maybe get your help on something."

"Okay, John Henry. Let me put my fish on ice 'till I can filet them."

Clay and Indian Joe sat at Joe's little breakfast bar and sipped cold beer while Clay told him all about his deal with the CIA seven years ago.

"So you see, Joe, the Agency is after me and I don't want a big fuss about it, but I have to defend myself until I can get in on Clayton Elliot."

"Then let's go zap 'em, John Henry."

"The trouble with that, Joe, is they'd just send five or ten more. No, I need to get myself two or three days, Man, to find Elliot and kill him."

"This ain't like you, Major. Those guys are after you and you need to take steps to "off" 'em."

"I don't have a problem with that, Joe, but I can't "off" every man in the Agency. I think if I can "do em" and keep the bodies from being found for a few days I can stop this shit from happening."

"Whatta you got in mind, John Henry?"

"I'd like to police 'em up, put 'em in their car and run it off in that real deep canal along I-95 west of Palm Beach."

"Let's go do it."

"You don't have any qualms?"

"Hell no! John Henry. I know the man that killed the chief is dead, but the agency ordered it and now they've sent killers after you. No! I have no qualms whatsoever. Let's go get 'em."

"Right. Now here's what we have to do. We have to go down to Fort Lauderdale, get them, put them in the back of their car and drive them back to Palm Beach, get on I-95 and go south. Then we pull off, put them in the front car, one driver and one passenger. We put the driver's foot on the accelerator with the car in neutral with the motor rev-ing. Then we reach in and pull the gear shift down into drive."

185

He went on, "Maybe we can pour some whiskey over them and throw the half empty bottle in the car with them. Then I walk south until you pick me up. See any problems?"

Indian Joe started laughing. "John Henry, that's damn near as perfect a plan as I've heard of," and he laughed some more.

When he finally stopped laughing he said, "These guys are old aged winos, aren't they?"

"Negative, Joe. These guys are first line CIA killers and that's the reason we have to kill them."

"Okay, Major. Just checking, but listening to your plan I figured they must be underage boy scouts."

"I didn't say they'd be easy, Joe. If they were easy the Russians would have gotten them all by now."

"John Henry, if we can capture them we can probably make it look like an accident by shooting them up with pure alcohol. Your plan of throwing some on them wouldn't work because the canal water would wash it all off and there'd be none in their blood stream."

"How do you shoot 'em up Joe?" John Henry asked.

"We use a syringe and plain, ol' hundred proof vodka. We slap it in their veins until they pass out. Then we've got about an hour to get them into the water to 'drown' before they die from the alcohol."

"Where do we get a syringe?"

"No sweat. I just happen to have an extra," and he commenced laughing again.

"Joe, don't worry. I'm not gonna be asking anything more about that."

"They got a few things from Joe's cabin, put his fish in the freezer after gutting them, and headed east to Fort Lauderdale in Clay's little "rice-burner" car.

They arrived in Fort Lauderdale and drove through the motel's parking garage where John Henry quickly spotted the white agency sedan. They started looking for an empty slot to pull into when Joe suddenly said, "Major, look!"

Two men, definitely agency, were getting into the white sedan. John henry drove the circle in the garage and was right behind the white sedan when it pulled out of the parking garage and turned west toward I-95.

On I-95 going north Clay stayed two or three cars back and followed them off the exit ramp to Bal Cove. They headed east and Clay followed, allowing quite a bit of distance between them.

They entered Bal Cove and Clay followed them almost to his own home.

They parked about a half a block from his house and sat there for about ten minutes as they were apparently watching it.

One got out finally, straightened his tie, and tugged his jacket down where it had pulled up over his Uzi rig under his arm. He started walking toward Clay's house, probably to check if Clay was home or not.

Clay took his extra set of handcuffs and eeled out of his car and by the time the agency man had gotten almost to Clay's house Clay was opening the door to the agency sedan, the .32 held in front of him.

Joe reached in the other side about the same time and reached under the man's jacket and snaked the Uzi out. Clay slapped cuffs on him, then dragged him out of the car and did a quick frisk, and found a duplicate of his own little .32 He gave it to Joe who put it in his belt behind his jacket.

He had Joe take the CIA Agent back to his car. Then he took the man's place in the sedan, and waited for the other agent to return.

A few minutes later he saw the other agent returning and he was taking long strides. Evidently Mary Beth had gone somewhere and had left the garage door open, so the man knew Clay wasn't at home.

Clay idly scratched his head as the agent neared the car, conveniently covering his face, until the agent stooped, opened the door and stopped, shock on his face.

Clay motioned him to stand still, then Joe slipped behind him and pulled out his "fangs": another Uzi and a short barrel .38 caliber police special.

They handcuffed him and put him in the sedan. Then Clay pulled the sedan around and stopped next to his own car. The first agent they had captured was in the back seat, inconscious.

Clay asked, "What happened, Joe?"

Joe laughed and showed Clay a bloody red laceration on his forehead and the side of his head. "He liked to killed me with those cuffs, Major. I had to cold-cock him with his own pistol."

They put him in the front seat between John Henry, who was going to drive the sedan, and the other prisoner. They agreed to pull off into the south bound side rest area just north of West Palm Beach. They would "sedate" the prisoners there, some five miles from where they planned to send the white sedan into the canal.

An hour later, about dark, both cars were parked in the darkest area of the rest area parking lot. The one agent was still unconscious. Clay was a little worried about it but then realized he was going to kill them anyway.

They were killers who had been recruited for exactly that purpose by the agency. Not killing them would expose not only himself but Mary Beth and the children, for the agency's compartmented system of mission assignments would mean these two would report back only to their assigning office. In this case Clay was sure it was Clayton Elliot.

No, these two had to die for if he got Elliot and they remained alive they would bring the entire agency down on him and his family. Don't get soft and sentimental, he told himself.

At ten o'clock Clay and Joe gave the shots—twenty CCs of vodka into the vein of the one who was awake. Five CCs into the vein of the unconscious one.

Clay told Joe to leave five minutes after him and follow to pick him up. He removed the cuffs and replaced their weapons then got in the sedan and headed south. He knew the exact spot where he wanted to do it and pulled out behind a long string of cars.

He pulled off the road and pointed the nose of the car down the slope toward the canal. The one in the passenger side was already belted in and he pulled the agent from the middle into the driver's seat and buckled him in.

Not a car had passed but he hurried anyway. He pushed the drivers' side agent's foot down on the accelerator causing the sedan motor to roar. Leaving lights on he reached in the window and snapped the gear shift down into drive. The sedan leaped forward throwing him sideways.

He picked himself up, rubbing his right shoulder where the car had grazed him in its terrible leap forward, then down through the few bushes to nose its way into the black waters of the canal.

Both head lights were still glowing in the fifteen foot deep canal even after the bubbles and commotion finally died down.

As he watched, the lights flickered and died out and the only sounds to be heard were from the mosquitoes humming and a few calls from the night birds.

189

He staggered up the slope of the road way and started walking south. One car passed when Joe stopped and he got in.

"How'd it go, Major?" he asked.

"Joe, killing those two like that is about the roughest thing I've ever done."

"John Henry, you had to do it. There was no other way. You have to wonder how many people these two have eliminated over the years for your asshole CIA man Elliot."

"You're absolutely right, Joe. I had no choice, but now I've got to do the main job."

TWENTY-THREE

"For the wages of sin is death."
Romans vi 23

John Henry left his automobile at the small motel in Springfield, Virginia and caught an express bus into downtown Washington. His target was CIA headquarters in their new building in Fairfax, Virginia.

He was unshaven and wore old clothes. Deep wrinkles lined his face. He had bushy eye brows.

In his pocket was a gray wig and a set of plain glass horn rim glasses. The fedora hat that he was wearing completed his disguise.

He went into an unattended parking lot and found a large sedan, some five years old, with many dents and scratches.

It would have taken him two seconds to pop the door, but he didn't need to as the left rear door was unlocked.

Clay walked to the front of the car and ran his hand inside the front bumper and found the magnetic box that held the spare key. It was dirty and covered with mud. The owner had probably long since forgotten he had put it there.

The key fit and the motor turned over and purred like a well-fed kitten. The owner had kept the car running well

191

but had ignored the appearance. Considering the high crime record of the Washington D.C. area this was probably good thinking.

Clay drove fifteen blocks to CIA Headquarters in Fairfax, not indicated as CIA Headquarters of course, but the Import-Export company sign fooled no one, least of all foreign agents.

He stopped about a block away, put the wig on and replaced his hat. The plain glass eye glasses completed the transformation from a forty-seven-year-old man to an old man at least in his seventies.

He entered the front of the huge parking lot, the part not within the chain link barrier, and there was plenty of space. It was just a few minutes before six P.M. and in the two days Clay had scouted the place Clayton Elliot had exited the front entrance and walked to a waiting limo at exactly six P.M.

Today, however, the limo was drawn up closer to the building sidewalk, and there was no space to cut past him on the right. Clay timed it to the second and since there were no posts or obstructions, his right side wheels were on the sidewalk itself and the two left tires on the driveway.

Clayton Elliot came out from the building, took three steps and heard the roaring of the big engine of Clay's "borrowed car." He had floored the accelerator so the big car was doing sixty when it hit Elliot and threw him up into the air. He came down and landed on the hood, his staring eyes and face against the windshield.

Clay twisted the wheel and Elliot's body flew off. John Henry never looked back. Witnesses interviewed later said it was a real old man who probably had not even noticed he had run onto the sidewalk and killed the Director of Operations for the Import-Export business.

192

John Henry shed his disguise as he drove back toward the parking lot where he had stolen the car. To get it back without anyone being the wiser was sheer luck but he pulled the car into the same slot, got out and replaced the key. He checked the damage. There was only a faint crease in the hood and a little blood on the bumper and grill. He quickly wiped it off and stuck the bloody handkerchief in his front pocket for disposal. It was 1820 hours, or 6:20 PM and Clay had "used" the car for only 35 minutes.

He shuffled away and stood at a bus stop for ten minutes for a Shirley Highway bus to Springfield.

Back at his motel room Clay separated all the evidence the Chief had gathered against the CIA in their drug smuggling.

He had made five copies of everything and he carefully wiped each sheet and print and even the manila envelopes he was mailing them off in.

He had a package going to each of the three major wire services. The other two went to the New York Times and the Washington Post.

The next morning he drove to Washington and at a small branch post office weighed and mailed one packet. Then he bought the same amount of postage for the other packets. He affixed the postage to each packet then stopped at four different boxes and mailed them as he drove south.

When the papers came out the next day there was only a small blurb about a hit and run accident in which a high ranking officer of the Import-Export company was killed in front of their corporate headquarters. The report was buried on the fourth page of the Post and no name was given.

John Henry checked the obituary page. There it was. Clayton E. Elliot, Age 47, had died suddenly in an automobile accident. No other information was given.

Several days went by. One TV news station had a brief report about accusations that the CIA had run drugs into the LA area during the 80's. But that one broadcast and a story in the San Jose "Mercury," a newspaper on the west coast, was all that came of it.

Clay was not surprised at it being hushed up, and as he told Chico a few days later when he and Mary Beth were dining at Chico's beautiful restaurant in Miami, "The chief's killer is dead and the CIA man who ordered it is dead, and I'm sure a lot of underlings in the Agency have had reprimands placed on their records. So now I salute our comrade in arms, the chief. Rest in Peace, amigo."